Five Million Stories

THE BEST INTERNATIONAL SHORT STORIES FROM THE OMSCWP

CONTENTS

INTRODUCTION

SIMON MILLION

So here we are, almost six years since we published our first submission. In that time we have seen stories from every continent, from writers for whom English is not their first language, but for whom it is a global language.

And this collection will take you around the globe, through the strange and unusual other countries of our writer's minds, where you will encounter their interests, their fears, fascinations and insights. We have filtered and refined the blizzard of words and now present this fine collection for your entertainment.

The stories start in North Carolina, in tobacco growing country, and visit California too, but our trajectory will take us right around the globe to Pakistan, Afghanistan, to the great city of London, from the distant past through now to a future hidden from us for the time being.

You can travel in time and space with these authors. Let them be your guides to distant places through the fabulous medium of the short story.

Keep a hold of this book. There are names in here you will read again, perhaps on the spine of a book in your local store, maybe on a blog, perhaps in the newspaper, who knows?

Wait no more, read on...

The Devil Wind

Robert Watts Lamon

It was the late Nineties, when Westbrook Ames, editor of the *Big City Review*, sent me south. He wanted a story on the declining tobacco market and its effects on the family farms in the Tobacco Belt. And so, not long after I left his office, I was living in a rented farmhouse in rural North Carolina and getting to know the people living in the surrounding countryside.

Then came that weather quirk. It's been described in newspapers and televised documentaries. They told of a volcanic fissure deep in the Pacific Ocean that warmed the water and put a wrinkle in the storm track, causing the air to come spilling down from the upper altitudes. The odd densities produced a wind with an unprecedented sound—a deep sorrowful moan. It sounded as though the door to purgatory had been left ajar.

In early spring, I dug a garden patch in a small corner of the field behind the house and tended it loyally, when I wasn't writing or on the road. I was overjoyed to see the seedlings popping up. By late April, the corn was several inches high, squash and cucumber plants had broken through the orange crust, and I was feasting on lettuce and radishes.

One day, around that time, I was putting in tomato plants. It was a cloudy day and fairly mild—ideal for transplanting, except for that moaning wind. I had about twenty plants in the ground, when I heard a voice behind me.

"You'll have tomatoes by the Fourth of Ju-ly."

I turned to find my neighbor, Sam Dowd, in his bib overalls and baseball cap, glancing over my garden with a critical eye. He had thick limbs and a lively manner, though his face sagged and bore the wattles of age.

"Hear that mess last night?" he asked.

"Heard a truck," I replied.

"Crowd was tearing up Jim Davis's soybeans."

"Really?"

"Drove a four-wheel across his field."

"Who?"

"Jim said it was people from town."

"Bad crowds are getting bigger."

I had heard about a rash of thefts and vandalism— tractor stolen, tobacco shed burned, pigs let loose, farm ponds fouled with trash and dead cats, tire tracks spun into front yards,

"Somebody mad at Jim?" I asked.

"Naw—it was done out of pure meanness. Like running over a turtle."

Sam waved his hand and walked back across the neighboring field to his tractor.

I had finished transplanting and was knocking the dirt of my shoes, when I heard the tractor sputter and stall. Sam called out something in his resonant drawl. I hurried toward the field and saw his tractor lying on its side, with him lying next to it without his hat, which now lay ten feet away. I ran and stumbled across the plowed field. It had begun to drizzle, and scud clouds were chasing each other across the sky.

Sam's left leg was pinned under a big rear wheel of the tractor. I put my shoulder to the other big wheel and pushed hard and he pulled his leg free.

"Can you move the leg?" I asked.

"Ain't broke—my knee hurts some."

Sam managed to stand up, as his wife, Melanie, came hurrying across the field. The years had been kind to her—she was a handsome woman. As she approached, her cotton dress bounced and blew and showed her thighs.

"Sam—what in the world?" she said, short of breath.

"Front wheels hit something. Tractor rolled all of a sudden."

"Can you walk all right?"

Sam limped back and forth a few times and then spoke up. "Thanks neighbor. I'll send my two boys over here with a winch. They'll pull this thing back on its wheels—come on, Melanie, let's go home."

Sam was still limping as he walked away with Melanie beside him. I lingered near the overturned tractor, wondering what it had struck. It had been moving along ground sloping to its right. Then, as Sam said, it suddenly stopped and rolled. Good thing the ground was soft, or Sam's leg might have been in far worse shape. My first guess was that the tractor had hit a small sinkhole. But at the spot where it had stopped, I noticed a smooth, half-buried object. I dug around it with my foot, then with my bare hands, and revealed a chunk of concrete. I tried to move it, guessing its weight to be about a hundred pounds. I found a similar fragment nearby, then another, then another, all buried just beneath the surface. I had to conclude that the field had been sabotaged. As soon as I got back to the house, I telephoned Sam Dowd and astonished him with news of what I had discovered.

After lunch, I drove to the town of Leafland, North Carolina, just a collection of bungalows, along with a grain elevator, a sawmill, and a few stores, all scattered along the railroad tracks. I stopped at the laundromat and then, with clean clothes in the trunk, I rode to the grocery store. In the parking lot, I noticed some unkempt young men and a few careless young women loafing near the store entrance. I didn't like the look of them and perhaps made it too obvious by my expression. As I walked to the store, one of the men got between me and the door.

"Ain't you that queer?" he said. "The one that lives up yonder--near Sam Dowd?"

I looked him up and down, but said nothing. I had seen him once or twice, driving a tractor on the main road. He looked awful now—unwashed, unshaven, overalls filthy, eyes framed in red. He had one of those idiotic haircuts—long on top, close on the sides—and I pitied the barber who had given it.

"Didn't you hear me, queer?"

I still wouldn't answer this fool of a boy trying to impress his friends and those dull women hovering around him. I surprised him by grabbing the straps of his overalls and throwing him aside. A bully who had misjudged his man, he was stuck with the choice of backing down, or attacking and suffering defeat. He turned his attention to the wind blowing past the eaves and chimneys of the nearby buildings.

"Hear that?" he said meekly. "They say that's the sound of the Devil. Do you believe it?"

"The Devil is where you find him," I replied and walked past him.

Inside the store, I found the butcher, shelf-stocker, bagger, and cashier, all in the person of Mary Jo Crankshaw. Her husband worked their farm while she tended the store. She wore a white apron over her blue jeans, and her pretty face was somewhat darkened with worry.

"That boy giving you trouble, Danby?" she asked as I chose a wheeled basket.

"He's got whatever's going around—maybe something in the water."

"Maybe something in the soul."

"Yes—"

"Somebody's burning tobacco sheds."

"I heard about one."

"Three last week."

"Cigarette Nazis?"

"Could be."

"Well—I'd better get my groceries."

I toured the store with a little cart, pushing its squeaky wheels over the wooden floor. I came to the meat counter, where Mary Jo was putting cuts of meat on trays.

"Mary Jo—I'll take that eye-of-the-round."

She took the roast out of the cooler and wrapped it. I wondered whether I should buy some shells for my shotgun. I had bought the gun some time ago—as sort of a friend in the wilderness—but I had never fired it and still wasn't sure I wanted it around.

I took the wrapped meat from Mary Jo, and we met again at the checkout counter. We spoke as she rang up my groceries and we both bagged them.

"Your family's had this store for quite a while," I said.

"About sixty years."

I glanced around at the open crates of produce with price tags stuck among the contents, at the antique coffee grinder, at the elongated grabber dangling from an upper shelf.

"Not as busy as we used to be," she said.

"Things change."

"We'll manage. We're right good at getting by."

"Know that crowd out front?"

"Been knowing their families for years. They don't usually act that way."

"Sheriff could move them away."

"They might come back and break a window—or worse."

I thought for a moment and then asked, "Do you still keep shells for a shotgun?"

"Keep some."

"How about double-ought for a twelve gauge?"

"I've got those."

As I reached home and turned into the gravel driveway, a man ran from behind the house and away up the road. I gave chase in my car, but he vanished in the scrub near the shoulder of the road. The back of the house wasn't damaged, except for a tear in the screen door. But I was glad I bought those shotgun shells.

After dinner, I found a book to read. The wind had picked up again, and as darkness fell, I could hear that wind's moaning and the metal chimney's rain cover turning, turning. I dozed over the book and then awakened to see an orange glow on the window. Even in the house, I could smell the wood smoke. Looking out the front door and across the road, I saw one of Sam's tobacco sheds on fire. The old shed was made of split logs and caulking, and the fire was well under way.

I called the Sheriff, who called the volunteer fire company, but by the time the firemen arrived, they could only flood the ruins. I met the Sheriff coming up the walk. In the glow of my porch light, his square face looked even grimmer than usual.

"See anybody around that shed—before the fire?" he asked.

"No—was it set?"

"I think so. The heat wasn't on."

"What's Sam going to do?"

"He's got another shed to cure tobacco."

"Who's doing this?"

"All sorts."

"Why?"

"They just want to, I guess."

He stared at the ruined shed for a while and then, without another word, walked slowly to his patrol car. I was left thinking maybe that fool of a farm boy was right.

It was five days later that my editor called. Westbrook Ames was widely respected, but not for his patience.

"Danby?—look, Danby, what's going on down there?"

"I faxed you a piece yesterday."

"Yeah—about that strange wind. And all that strange behavior."

"That's right."

"What's that got to do with tobacco?"

"Plenty, I think—in a subtle way."

"Your assignment was tobacco—straightforward."

"I've interviewed farmers all over. I've spoken to manufacturing people. Tomorrow I'm visiting a warehouse in Wilson County."

"Things getting worse?"

"Sure—falling demand, competition from foreign growers, farmers looking for crops to replace tobacco. Many have left the farm altogether."

"Can you get me something by Monday?"

I had to check my calendar. Today was Wednesday. "I'll fax it to you late Friday."

"Good—say, why don't you get a laptop and a cell phone like the rest of the civilized world?"

"I like my Underwood—and my privacy."

"I'll be looking for that fax."

"Right."

Early the next day, I drove to Durham to visit a tobacco museum and then got back on the highway, reaching Wilson County in the early afternoon. I found the great wooden warehouse with its old beams and broad floor. I spoke to the owners and anybody else I bumped into. By that evening, I had the first draft of an article, and I spent the next day revising and fact checking. I got to the copy shop near closing and faxed my stuff to the *Big City Review*. The girl at the counter looked wide-eyed as she punched the numbers into the machine. I hoped Westbrook Ames would be equally fascinated.

It was a little past nine when I made the final turn toward home. As I approached my driveway, my little sedan was nearly sideswiped by a heavy-duty pickup truck. As it passed, I glimpsed the driver in my headlights. He was grinning--obviously pleased with himself. As Sam said, it was like running over a turtle.

After breakfast the next morning, I got into my gardening clothes and spent the rest of the forenoon planting more cucumbers and squash. I tried a few melons where the soil
was especially dark and moist. The sun climbed and warmed the ground. The surface became dry and crusty, and I stepped easily among the rows. Odd how the garden had become more important than Westbrook Ames and that damnable magazine.

Lunchtime came round, and I pulled off my shoes on the back steps. I made a salad from my home-grown greens and warmed some leftover beef. After the meal, I worked at my desk, making a series of notes on a yellow pad and placing them in a folder marked "Devil Wind," and then I returned to my garden. The early May sun was bright, and the earthy smells and the singing birds made my energy rise. Then I saw the people I would forever think of as gremlins.

The broad field surrounding my garden was covered with scrub. Beyond the field stood a pine woods. I noticed a group of people, perhaps six or seven, moving inside the tree line. They walked along the margin and then turned farther into the woods, and I lost sight of them. Past the woods, there was a pond and more clearing and some neighboring farms. I wondered what the gremlins were up to.

I heard gunfire. Were they firing at one another? Sometime later, I saw them again, returning by the same path. Apparently they hadn't lost anybody. They followed the tree line around the field to the road and disappeared over the next rise. Minutes later, a game warden stalked out of the same woods. He wore jodhpurs and tall hunting boots that made him look a character from a 1930s movie about forest rangers. He glanced back and forth as he walked toward me.

"Did you see that crowd?" he asked.

"Saw them coming and going."

"They were shooting."

"I heard."

"Shot a quail—out of season."

"Huh."

"Shot songbirds."

"Why don't you arrest them?"

"I will—when I catch up with them."

"I heard quite a few shots."

"They damaged some trees."

"Who are they?"

"Folks that ought to know better."

The despairing game warden walked back toward the woods. I left my garden for the day and, in the house, loaded my shotgun, checked the safety, and laid it carefully in the back of my closet.

June arrived and the weather turned hot. Kingbirds sat along the wires and fences and fed on the flies breeding in the pastures. Black beetles crawled across the yard, and wasps buzzed near my door. Working in my garden, I wore an aureole of gnats and struggled with the weeds springing up everywhere. Late one evening, after spending a long day pulling up weeds, I heard voices coming across the field behind the house. I thought the gremlins might be back. I looked out the back door and noticed shadowy figures moving among the trees. Still later, about to turn in, I took another look out back. As I stood in the doorway, a bullet cracked the air, coming so close I could feel its warm breeze. Then another came crashing through the kitchen window. I found the jagged circle in the glass and the hole in the opposite wall.

I got my shotgun from the closet, cocked it, and returned to the back door. There were human figures in the field near my garden. Their numbers grew, as though they were materializing from pure shadow. I fired well over their heads. The explosion fixed their attention— they stopped moving. Then they fled, melting away in the scrub, and that was the last I saw of them.

The wind was still loud when I awoke the next morning. The day was otherwise bright and clear, and I put on clean clothes and hiked over to Sam Dowd's farmhouse. I wanted to talk over my previous night's adventure. The fescue in his yard was bright green and neatly trimmed, and near the house, a big oak tree gave shade. I knocked on Sam's door, but got no response, so I walked past the house to the weathered barn.

"Sam—anybody here," I called as I stood at the barn door.

I saw someone moving inside the barn. A man—not Sam—jumped out the back window. I entered the crude air of the barn and walked back to the window the stranger had used for an exit. I heard a woman's voice. It came from the loft.

"Danby? Is that you down there?"

It was Melanie's voice. I walked up the wooden steps through the ceiling. In one corner of the loft, the hay was stacked halfway up the wall. Lying in the hay, naked except for a thin covering of straw, was Melanie.

She spoke with an eerie gaze. "Come lie with me, Danby. Sam's gone to town."

I was shocked, hypnotized—her flesh was still attractive. My mouth went dry, but then I bolted, stumbling down the wooden steps, hurrying out the wide barn door. I was halfway to the road, when I heard Melanie's voice behind me.

"Danby—you come back here."

I stopped and looked back. She was standing in the barn doorway, still naked, with arms akimbo. Then, suddenly, the moan in the wind faded and was gone. The quiet breeze was gentle on my face. Melanie's head fell forward. She covered herself with her hands and slouched back inside.

"I'm sorry, Danby," I heard her sob.

I turned away and walked home to my garden.

The volcanic fissure under the Pacific Ocean had sealed itself. The unique wrinkle in the storm track disappeared, and so did that moaning wind and the rife meanness that had come with it. Yes—bad things still happened in and around Leafland, from time to time, but they no longer clustered. I was going to call Westbrook Ames and, as they say, pitch another article about the strange wind and its effects on the locals. But then I just thought the hell with it and wrote the article and faxed it along with the stuff he wanted.

In the minds of some, the "Devil Wind" became associated with evil deeds— through simple coincidence. But then, the wind became prophecy. It provided an excuse to slip the ties that bind and revel destructively in a dying tobacco world. At least, that's the explanation I sent to Westbrook Ames. Even if he didn't publish it, I thought it might register on his calcified editor's brain.

He and I

Claire E Bluett

He refuses to eat: black olives, mushrooms, meat off the bone. I am like a human garbage disposal – I'll eat almost anything, with the exception of brussel sprouts, which he loves roasted with garlic.

He hates to drive, and prefers to ride his bicycle on errands even on the hottest afternoons and the coldest, darkest winter nights. This is admirable and brave and environmentally conscious. I am frightened of bicycles, and prefer the illusion of safety the car provides, along with its climate control capabilities. On those occasions that he does drive, he curses the other drivers and shifts gears forcefully, causing the car to buck and stall. He would rather take the bus.

He is thrifty and value-conscious. When we walk through any grocery store, he knows whether the price of any particular item is a good one and what the same item costs at all the rival stores. I follow along, taking his word for it even though I cannot imagine how he keeps all of that information stored.

But I have no reason to doubt him. He has an encyclopedic mind. His vocabulary is intimidating in its breadth and variety. All the time I ask him meanings of words I don't recognize or quite understand. He answers without hesitation or error. I find scraps of paper covered with handwritten words and their meanings tucked inside the books I borrow from him.

Where I like to think of myself as well read, he actually is. He reads classic works in his spare time: A Picture of Dorian Gray, Great Expectations, Dangerous Liaisons, Lord Jim. I read Chelsea Handler, Nicholas Sparks and other less meaningful works as assigned by a ladies' book club.

He is meticulous and covetous of his things – however inexpensive or replaceable. He insists I take care not to break the binding on borrowed books, or to crumple the pages of the magazines he harvests from the dumpster at work. Once, I let my sister borrow a set of DVDs. I didn't ask his permission, even though technically they are his since he bought them. He likes my sister, but still warned that "they had better not get messed up" when I told him I loaned them out.

He cries when famous people die, and at the end of sad movies.

We both love karaoke. Actually, it is because of him that I love it. One of our first dates was to a karaoke night at a bar. He went wild on stage, singing with abandon and executing high kicks at appropriate times. I, lingering near the bar and calming my nerves with kamikazes, was amazed. I learned that a karaoke superstar need not be able to sing, only to perform. Now, we wow audiences with our impassioned, off-key duets.

Most of the music I like now he introduced me to.

Most of the books I like now he let me borrow.

I wanted to be a good photographer, perhaps less so for the art of it than the accoutrements. The lenses and straps and cases of a photojournalist all seem to carry the weight of importance and convey a compelling need to document life in all it's beauty and savagery. I took a photography class at the university where I studied, and ended up changing my major because I could not pass the course. The f-stops and shutter speed and aperture were as foreign to me as calculus. I lacked the patience required to develop film and suffered panic attacks inside those tiny, dark closets reserved for loading exposed film onto reels for developing.
Even if I could master the mechanics of it, I could never be good at it. I will never have the requisite artistic eye. It is a source of great failure to me.

He of course, mastered it. He too studied it, but with much greater success. His professors admired his talent and invited him to photograph their soirees. At some point, his interest, or his confidence, waned. He packed away his cameras and film and buried his photographs deep inside the boxes lining his closets. I don't understand why someone so good at something so elusive would give it up so completely and without a second thought. I am jealous of his ability to do this – to learn and be good at one thing, and then leave it and move on to the next.

But he is a patient person, and deliberate. He enjoys the process as much as the product. I prefer instant gratification. I hurry to complete a task, relying on gut and ingenuity more than method and craft. I like to demolish.
He likes to create.

He constructs piles of books, magazines, notebooks, sections of old newspapers and photocopies of interesting drawings and articles on every flat surface of the bedroom.
He arranges and rearranges them according to some system only he knows. At first I thought he kept these things in piles for lack of space to store them. I purchased shelves and made room in spare closets for him. Now I know they are a permanent fixture in his life, and so, in mine.

He is a collector by nature. Every closet in the house is filled with comics, books, CDs and records. He maintains a mental inventory of these things and knows exactly where to find an item he hasn't seen in years. I have trouble remembering where I place my keys or glasses or wallet.

He picks up scrap paper he finds on the ground, hoping to find some odd insight in a stranger's shopping list or discarded note. Once he found a spiral notebook filled with the bad poetry of some adolescent girl. The junior-high emotion of it tickled me, and I made snide remarks about the pages filled with rhyming laments about the unfairness of love and friendship. But he was touched by it, and understood what I had forgotten: that every one of us once felt the same way. I regretted my insensitivity. I am sure he kept the notebook, in a stack somewhere in our bedroom.

He is better at parallel parking than I am.

He knows how to draw and I don't.

He has seen all the great movies I am just now getting around to watching. He knows the names of the actors and directors and can recite lists of other movies they've done.

The rhythm of his life is punctuated by the growth of his facial hair. He allows his beard to grow for months and then shaves it off, but is never clean-shaven for more than a day. The first time I saw him beardless I was surprised by his weak chin.

He hates parties or large gatherings of people. He will immediately find his way to a corner to sit, or else find me and tell me he is ready to leave. He is ready to leave almost from the time we arrive. I tell him we'll stay for one more drink, which turns into two and when we finally leave he is grumpy and ready for bed.

Two years ago, the husband of his good friend became gravely ill with cancer. It was a long illness, and in that time, he rarely spoke to his friend. When they did speak, he did not ask about Andrew's illness or if she was doing okay. I know this because I would ask him about it and grew frustrated by his inability to answer. I found it hard to understand why he didn't seem concerned about his friends. Of course, he was concerned, that is just his way. He lets people be, waits for them.

Four years ago, when we first met, I would wonder why so many days would pass between phone calls. Invariably, I would give in and call, wanting to talk to him, wanting to see him again. That is just my way. I seek people out, look for them.

He tells me he doesn't know what he'd do without me.

Mullah Radio

Emm Aye

The vintage black-box lying in the window of the renovated Stylish Saloon abruptly went into throes of an outrageous fits of cough. Then relaxed to regain breath stuck up in the pharynx before heaving another gigantic one. This was a chronic malaise and the keen eavesdroppers had learned to live with it. Although, the black-box had been a break-down candidate for eternity, a couple of spanks on either side always helped resuscitate it. So it had kept on coughing, going hyper and hypo in tandem, and spluttering mucus of melodies, news bulletins, sports commentary, and now Mullah Radio's evening harangues with tremendous tenacity. Tonight's mucus was real pervasive and venomous.

It was a walk dipped in fright; confusion.

Musa Khan carried the corpse on his right shoulder, and Isa Khan holding his father's left index finger sobbed sulkily. The harrowing specter of his missing out on John Cena beat the hell out of Dave Batista loomed large as an inescapable eventuality in his damp eyes. They did not talk to each other; the occasion did not necessitate it, too.

Both lost in a silent mechanical walk could reminisce a similar march to an identical destination a month ago when they transported the remains of their oldman in a funeral procession.

The news of the suicide blasts at *Loya Jirga* was shocking but not from the blue. Such fireworks had been pretty much in vogue in Swat Valley of late. The oldman and the *Loya Jirga*; there was a dialectical disconnect – he was not a Khan, a Malik, a Mullah or a Chieftain, but a mere barber – yet he aspired to be part of the process of raising a bulwark against the mounting menace of FM radio. The national hook-up put the casualty count at forty-five *numbers*; he was somewhere one of them. When whatever remained of him was received, Isa Khan reckoned, was good for a few dozen Peshawari *Chappal Kebabs* only.

Then men had ambled along carrying the casket right to the graveyard. This time they waited at the site of the final rites.

Pyre was ready at Green Chowk. They off-loaded themselves with heavy hearts to the impassioned congregation.

It was only the previous night that viewing TV had been declared *taghoot*. Mullah Radio, at length denounced the diabolical device, and dubbed it the root-cause of ever-increasing immorality and a tool of advancement of imperial agenda on the pious people; hence culpable. The edict ordained that all such profane appliances be put to fire the next evening. There was no mention of consequences for the non-compliant but that was not needed. Everybody understood FM radio edicts – both that were articulated and that were withheld.

The sinful responded in solemnity and droves.

Green Chowk burst into slogans of *Allah-o-Akbar* as fire ignited under the mountain of devious boxes. Pious Pupils leading the charge with bamboo rods viciously attacked the pyre with angst in eyes and toxin in tongues. They kicked, punched, and hammered any pieces of plastic falling sideways of the exploding hellfire; the on-lookers toed the line exhibiting piety and allegiance. Both the pious and the sinful released their rage in unison till the inferno cooled off alongwith remains of any vulgar visuals latent inside the vacuum tubes.

Mingora was cleansed of all immorality in a short span of one hour on that early spring evening. The sinful returned with their heads dropping down and divided between a simultaneous sense of loss and gain failing to decipher which one was their own. Musa Khan's eyes instinctively panned from the bonfire cheerleaders to the glittering *Stylish Saloon*, and then to Isa Khan – who was now lost in the excitement of the moment. He suddenly found himself at a cross-roads; a decision was required to be made.

Musa Khan and Kanwal had met on the faultlines of history.

It was a sunny winter morning when Kanwal – in skin-tight faded blue jeans, explosive red top and with bulges – struck Musa Khan like a thunderbolt. She had barged into Garm Hmam escorted by a bunch of glamorous boys and girls to extend him invitation for the *First National Barbers' Convention*, which her NGO was hosting in Peshawar to launch *Pilot Project for the Prevention of Hepatitis and AIDS through Awareness Raising and Capacity Building of Barbers in Hygiene and Safety Standards.*

'Figures show that every sixth adult and eighth child in Swat Valley is suffering from Hepatitis or AIDS or both, and the numbers are rising.' Kanwal contextualized her visit looking deep into Musa Khan's still eye-balls.

'Ok. Yes.' His tongue and mind had lost coordination.

'Study also indicates that large spread of these diseases may be attributable to the process in which men get their shaves and haircut. I am not blaming anybody. You people don't know yet. I mean the spread of these dangerous diseases could be controlled by learning and observing hygiene and safety best practices.' Kanwal stopped realizing it was getting too thick for the audience.

'Yes. Ok.' Musa Khan mumbled.

'So join us at the launching ceremony. It would be fun. Right?' Kanwal cut it short.

'Ok. Yes,' he murmured again.

Musa Khan mechanically kept waving to gusts of dust behind Kanwal's Cruising till the customer draped in the white-turned-grey towel shouted of the shaving cream applied on his face having gone dry.

He received much deserved second electric-shock at the convention in a five-star hotel in Peshawar a week later. He was awe-struck by the splendor of the event. Completely ignoring his community from other towns, he stood in a hypnotic daze with his eyes glued at the elevated dais. Kanwal wearing a beautiful dress glittering with shiny beads was gleefully seated alongside chief guest – the minister for health. Across was proudly perched Raja Abdul Rashid, *Chairman, All Pakistan Federation of Barbers' Associations.*

The speeches generally revolved around the hygiene and safety concepts, prevention of infections, deadliness of the diseases and to top all, the critical role of barbers towards their prevention. Musa Khan had an unusual feeling of being important and honored. The chairman, looking to exploit the event to advance his political agenda in the wake of Federation's upcoming elections, announced establishing *National Baldness R&D Fund* to sponsor research to overcome baldness in one year's record time which would result in substantial revenue increase for all barbers. The chief guest appreciated the program, and announced a support of five thousand rupees for the Fund.

Musa Khan was over the moon; Garm Hmam had been selected as the only implementing partner of the project from Mingora.

'She is gorgeous.' Musa Khan poked Samad Khan – a long-time friend – while boarding the bus bound for Mingora.

'I didn't think you were that stupid. I smack a rat here.' Samad Khan, still trying to overcome his failure to make it, alarmed him.

'Oh, really! How?'

'She is either a Jew or an American spy.'

'American spy?'

'Or she has some hidden political agenda.'

'What political agenda?'

'Elections! What else is political?'

'What elections?'

'President of *All Pakistan Federation of Barbers' Associations* – in place of Raja Abdul Rashid.'

'Look at your face! You think she is a barber like you and me?' Musa Khan broke into a loud laughter.

'You would see!' Samad Khan wriggled out of the spat looking out of the window.

Musa Khan got the needed leisure to frame Kanwal in various poses, interrupted only by the repeated security check-posts on the way. The journey was cut by the half.

Although, Pious Pupils had started using FM radio a few years ago, Mullah Radio's regular sermons were not audible in Mingora until the onset of spring. The earlier *taghoot* edicts – spread through word of mouth – pertained to banning of girls' attending schools, and boys' joining seminaries only. The non-compliant were not punished individually; everyday a school or two were blasted and razed to the ground.

On her first post-convention visit, Kanwal presented Musa Khan a brand new tool-kit packed in a fine leather-bag and a truckload of antiseptics. While she introduced new implements and their various functions, Musa Khan found his own tools shabby; humble. Kanwal's people enacted a role-play: a boy sat in the cutting-chair and a girl applied cream on his face and shaved him. Kanwal kept describing each minute detail of the process. Musa Khan was fascinated – a woman shaving a man. Kanwal also exhibited the desired way of washing hands by holding Musa Khan's hands palm to palm with fingers interlaced. He yearned time to halt. It did not and the hands slowly got disengaged. He also learned how to clean and sterilize his implements before putting them to next customer.

Life at Green Chowk would come to a halt upon Kanwal's arrival. Hawkers, drivers, pedestrians, and bus-commuters leaving for suburban localities would forget blinking as she would get down her Cruising and start the elegant march toward Garm Hmam. Musa Khan would suddenly emerge from nowhere with his eyes popping out to proudly receive his glamorous guests. It was quite an event in Green Chowk's otherwise dull, dusty and uninteresting life.

Musa Khan and Kanwal had suddenly arisen as the most talked-about twosome in Mingora – often displacing even Mullah Radio. There were infinite stories about Kanwal in circulation. 'She is American agent.' 'She is Pious Pupil's spy.' 'She has an affair with Musa Khan.' 'American drones cover her.' 'She is a Jew.' Samad Khan would rub all these theories into Musa Khan's ears repeatedly but only to be brushed aside.

This was a fairy-tale romance until the bonfire night.

While Kanwal was leaving after her next visit, Musa Khan engaged her.

'Situation is very bad here. They have now started operating in Mingora with freedom and without much resistance. People say shaving would be declared *taghoot.*'

'Musa Khan, I know it. But people don't know when you diminish from outside first you diminish from inside. They don't know what is happening to them. You don't worry. You be brave!'

'I have a small son; a family. I am worried.'

'Do you think opting out will make you any better? You will shut shop and go home? How will you feed your people? What about your son's schooling? You want him to join them one day? What will happen if everybody keeps surrendering? Don't you think I am also threatened; I am a woman. Come on be a man! There is talk of full military operation but nothing will succeed until you be a man yourself.' Musa Khan's face remained sullen while she patted him to mop up her visit. She knew what worked and when.

Next morning Mingora woke up to a horrifying specter. Ayub Khan was found hung to the electric pole in front of Stylish Saloon. He ran a video shop – a vocation declared *taghoot* a few days ago. Ayub Khan's blunder was to delay the closure. He took to off-loading stocks through loot-sale to retrieve some money to put up a fruit-cart. Musa Khan felt shattered. He was his regular customer. He rented adult movies for watching at Samad Khan's place.

Green Chowk got its alias – Khooni Chowk.

A couple of more meetings and both parties found themselves crossing the original terms of endearment. Kanwal having detected in Musa Khan a quality guinea pig started practically testing her Ivy League learnings in the tough terrains of Swat Valley. Musa Khan blindfolded raced down the steep hill where there was nowhere to stop – a halt and he would come down crashing.

Rickety *Garm Hmam* gave way to colorful *Stylish Saloon*. Time *7AM – 9PM* on the door was amended also to notify *Lunch break: 1PM – 2PM* in quest of exactitude. Soon a few more beautiful panels like *'Our Tools are Fully Sterilized'*, *'Political Conversation Prohibited'*, *'Work on Credit Not on Offer'*, *'Smoking Not Allowed Here,'* were found hanging at appropriate places inside Stylish Saloon.

While rumors of a *taghoot* edict against shaving grew rife, Musa Khan and his community started listening to Mullah Radio's evening harangues with regularity and respect like everybody else in Swat Valley. They would huddle around the black-box at Stylish Saloon after dusk, shutter-drop, carefully listen to the sermons and weigh their options. The bulletins now more audible – installation appeared to have moved closer to Mingora hills – were increasingly stuffed with updates on victories achieved by Pious Pupils against the infidel occupants of the neighboring holy lands, the demolition count of boys and girls schools, women lynched and stoned for sinful conduct, and fresh edicts of all sorts. Everybody felt relieved if no edicts concerning them were issued that night. Women's names were not called out of sanctity; they were just picked up to deliver punishments – like Zarina Khan who was stripped forty times in public for dubious demeanor.

'Living a fearful life isn't good for you,' Musa Khan's wife empathized after supper.

'Who the hell is living a fearful life? I am not afraid,' Musa Khan retorted having taken it to his manliness.

'In times like these it is good to be fearful.'

'Why should I be afraid? I am not committing a crime.'

'They think you are committing a sin.'

'Let them!'

'It isn't wise to stand up against the storm. Let it pass. Where barbers; where bravery! Think of your son. I beg you. Leave everything. Leave that witch. Let's move to the camp. We will return when it is peace,' she pleaded kneading his feet.

'It isn't about the witch, stupid,' Musa khan laughed.

'I know what these fashionable women can do. Don't you know the entire city talks about – you and her? Half of Mingora has fallen vacant. Let's go,' she persisted with her pleading.

'You want us to rot in the stinking camp like lakhs of other people. I would live and die here. I will not run like a coward. OK? I am a man.' He turned side and feigned asleep. He wanted to dwell with the sweet thought of people talking about – him and her.

It is dungarees time at Stylish Saloon.

Kanwal was over the moon to spot the transformation. She instinctively muttered: 'What if 'ISO-9001 certified' is also added up there?' and soon work on the assignment got underway.

While the black-box continued spluttering mucus against individuals one after the other – every night, and impelling more people to leave for refugee camps, movie-going was declared *taghoot*. All six three cinemas were clinically taken out over the next couple of nights.

Samad Khan confided to Musa Khan that the decision to ban shaving had been taken but was withheld to fully trap an enemy spy who was repeatedly visiting the area, and also to first cleanse the society of more serious ills.

Samad Khan ominously proved right.

Next morning the news of Palwasha Khan's murder overwhelmed Mingora. Both of them felt rocked. They had been to her attic to see her dance. 'She was a dazzling woman.' Musa Khan thought and let his imagination fly to its usual destination of late. In the afternoon, Samad Khan helped disperse the awaiting crowd by informing that Palwasha Khan's body would not be hung in Khooni Chowk to avoid exhibiting a female figure.

Khooni Chowk was fast becoming a haunted crossing.

With tourism having become relic of the olden times, Musa Khan's strict observance of work-timing, wearing dungarees, exchanging courtesies with clients, and to top all, his reputation of sterilizing his tools, proved automatic adverts; revenue-boosters.

Kanwal was no less a crowd-puller herself. Stylish Saloon would soon get jam-packed upon her arrival. She would monitor how safety standards were observed and freely interact with the customers. She passionately hugged an oldman who refused to sit in the cutting-chair unless razor-blade had first been replaced; supply had created its own demand. Kanwal was enthralled to see the silent change take place. She made friends with Isa Khan who – with no TV at home and school bombed – now spent much of his time helping his father.

Stylish Saloon continued to be measured for ISO-9001.

While expectations for a full operation fast built up, military still held past Churchill's Picket.

Musa Khan ended up reinvesting substantial revenues to transform the out-lying muddy patches into a parking lot. He laid off workers who failed to consecrate to safety standards and conduct professionally. Stylish Saloon swallowed the next shop and put in place a system of prior appointments to avoid rush. It also started serving welcome *Chai* to the clients. Musa Khan required of the competing kiosks to buy new kettles and cups, and ensure cleanliness, and proper service.

Summer had started to set in when Kanwal broke the propitious news of Stylish Saloon having qualified for ISO-9001, and also won the program's best implementer award. A befitting ceremony was required to grace him with the honors; an on-site event was planned for the purpose.

An evening before the event, the black-box spluttered a lump of poisonous mucus; Mullah Radio delivered *taghoot* edict against shaving. The impact was massive; instant. All barbers shutter-dropped immediately and vanished.

Musa Khan consulted Kanwal and did neither.

While space in front of Stylish Saloon was being cleared and pavilions installed, Pious Pupils took a round of Khooni Chowk in an open jeep brandishing weapons. They halted to take note of the activity as well of Stylish Saloon. Musa Khan's heart missed a beat or two. Samad Khan whispered to him: 'Look they are here. She is not. She will not. It is a trap Musa Khan. Take your family. You still have time. Go my friend! Go!' Musa Khan's face was sallow. 'But there is still full one hour to go. She is not taking her phone but those are jammed in the whole area. She would come.' 'Damn her! Shut it down. Run.' Samad Khan almost shouted at him. In the meantime, somebody hurried up and whispered in Samad Khan's ears ... 'What? Oh, my God! My shop blasted? I shutter-locked it ever since. Musa Khan it is a clue for you! I go and have a look at it; I come back. But Musa Khan you go. Time is fast running out for you.' He scurried into the city like a ghost.

Except sparse vehicles emitting smoke-full chants, a macabre lull prevailed over Mingora.

When Samad Khan returned, Musa Khan's body was hung with the power-pole right over the freshly-prepared dais in front of Stylish Saloon. Kanwal was not there. A large crowd stood by to watch the specter. In a remote corner, holding his own trembling hands, Isa Khan cried helplessly. A couple of Pious Pupils armed to the teeth gave guard to the corpse to ensure it received full punishment of hanging for a day and a night.

While the crowd held back their breath, a bruised tigress in faded blue jeans and provocative top emerged from nowhere and scrambled through the crowd straight to the guarding Pious Pupils. She grabbed them by the collar with each hand and shook them with ultimate contempt. 'You killed him. You killed him. He saved people's lives. Look at them. They are sick. They are dying of Hepatitis and AIDS and now you. You are sick and you are dying, too. He was a better man. He earned legitimate living, educated his son, and saved peoples' lives.' One Pious Pupil jerked to get his collar free and frowned. 'He disobeyed *taghoot* edict. He sinned.' She slaps the Pious Pupil with maximum power and disdain. 'You talk of sin. I talk of crime!' The other Pious Pupil shouts: 'Will of Allah shall prevail,' straightens his Kalashnikov and pulls the trigger. While a sprout of hot red blood springs from her mid-section, she roars at the highest pitch of her voice: 'Yes ... but through the will of these people ...', and goes down motionless.

People scramble for shelter. Isa Khan runs, returns, pulls off his award and ISO-9001 from Kanwal's blood-soaked hands and vanishes with the escaping flock.

In the evening, two bodies were hung side by side with the power-pole in Khooni Chowk. The fresh one was wrapped in a black *burqa* – out of sanctity for women.

First Blood

Marian Brooks

Jenna

It is a perfect day to clean out the refrigerator. There's almost nothing in it except for eggs, one quart of 2% milk, orange juice, brie and a seaweed salad purchased at Costco. The demonstrator swore that it had very few calories and could cure almost anything from headaches to foot fungus. While the sample tasted OK at the store, neither of us could bring ourselves to eat it later on.

Jack and I have similar tastes in most things, the more peculiar the better. I love that about him.

As I wipe the shelves clean, I notice a vial of red liquid stuffed behind the milk carton. It looks most certainly like blood. But whose? My short-term memory has been full of holes lately but surely I would have recalled putting any kind of bodily fluid into the fridge.

There are several pair of latex gloves under the kitchen sink. I slip on a pair of the purples, lift the tube out of the refrigerator with my thumb and forefinger and hold it up to the florescent lights. Nothing looks like blood, except blood. I should know. I've been an ER nurse for fifteen years.

2

My new husband has settled into the brown recliner and is now half-asleep. He looks so still, I wonder if he's breathing. He often looks like he's sleeping even when he's walking, not unlike those globules in the lava lamps he likes to collect. I think this discovery is important enough to rouse him. I pull on his big toe and shout, "Jack, Jack. Look at this! I think its blood! It was in our refrigerator."

A tall, thin man with an undecided moustache, Jack emerges slowly from the confines of the chair. His back has been hurting lately. He replies, "Yes, yes, I know. I thought we'd celebrate our first anniversary with a Bloody Mary." He smiles broadly, pulls me close and nuzzles my neck. At first I feel my heart racing and then, an unpleasant sting. I flinch and push him away. Jack whispers, "I wanted to surprise you, Jenna."

Later, I waken to the sight of my own blood, so red, so startling, I think about how simple it would be to just surrender. Spellbound, I watch, as my body's ink begins to write its very own story all over the Egyptian cotton pillow case. I must do something soon. All the seaweed in the world is not going to help me now.

I decide not to die

3

I'm weak and very confused. As popular as vampires seem to be these days, I can't be married to one. Besides, Jack likes garlic in his spaghetti sauce and doesn't sleep in a coffin. We play tennis on sunny days and he hasn't yet turned into a pile of ash. I can guarantee that there are no black capes in his closet.

Quietly, I drag myself out of bed, throw the pillow case into the washer and bandage the wounds. They're all too real. I pull a turtle neck sweater over my head, hiding the damage to my neck.

Then, I tip-toe around looking for Jack. He's back in that recliner on the first floor as if nothing has happened. The Phillies are at bat on our new flat screen TV. He's cursing at the manager.

Jack

About five hundred years ago, I decided that I would retire in the year 2012. There were all kinds of predictions about The Rapture (whatever that is) and, according to the Mayan calendar, world destruction is only days away. I was a loner, rarely hunted with a pack, never aspired to be an Alpha, too much responsibility. Retirement is a little known option for those of us who can choose to live forever. Most seem to want to go on and on. Not me, although I did manage to get into some beautiful mischief at times. I've had it with the perpetual search for voluptuous and willing throats even though the internet has made the process almost seamless.

So, I applied for a small pension from *The Undead Society* and was released from my contract. It was easier than I thought. I was no longer affected by the sun and didn't need a cape. I do carry a cane though. All those years of bending over swooning maidens has damaged my back permanently. I've grown quite fond of garlic too. I will have to die, however, but not at the hands of some religious zealot who wants to plunge a stake into my heart. That's just a myth anyway. One of the terms of agreement includes a stipulation that I turn in my cape and swallow one eight ounce glass of blood annually; some kind of maintenance schedule like rotating my tires. At this stage, I'm hardly a flight risk.

Jenna is a cautious, no-nonsense kind of woman. She looks like a bookish little barn owl when she turns her head and blinks. Very rarely, she wears really high heels and neon headbands, completely out of character. We've been married for a year now. In fact it's our first anniversary today. We met at a whiskey bar in Philadelphia and bickered about who was going to pay the tab for the drinks. Sometimes love grows out of a squabble. Of course, she had no idea about any of this or she wouldn't have married me. She's too smart to be caught dead with someone who owns an eccentric history like mine. I feel a little guilty about today; pulling her into my own dark orbit. I nipped her neck playfully and she passed out. There wasn't really that much blood, in fact, just enough.

6

I hear Jenna opening the refrigerator. The vial of blood is long gone but resting smack in the middle of the shelf is a large Red Velvet cake; one black candle in the center. "Happy Anniversary to Us," I wrote. There are white orchids and a small jewelry box on the table. My wife smiles warmly. Already she's forgetting.

END

I Had a Bone

Allen Kopp

August had to look away as his father and Mrs. Bone moved around the dance floor, weaving in and out among the other fools. It was too ridiculous. His father, looking like an undertaker in his conservative blue suit, clutched her to him as if he thought she might get away if he loosened his grip. Something about them as a pair was all out of proportion. He was six inches taller than she was, but her hips were wider and she had enormous arms as if she wrestled alligators in her spare time. She wore spike heels in which she had trouble walking and a red dress with an inch or so of cleavage. She wasn't a young woman. August felt embarrassed for her.

When they returned from their dance, father held her chair out for her and then sat down himself. Quite the dashing fellow.

"Oh, my!" Mrs. Bone said. "That was fun, wasn't it? We need to do that more often!" She picked up her martini and gulped it down.

"Not as young as I once was," father said, breathing heavily and straightening his tie.

Mrs. Bone took a cigarette out of her bag; father lit it for her dutifully. "Would you like to dance with me, August?" she asked.

"I don't know how," he said.

"I can show you. It's easy."

"No, thank you."

"You need to learn *sometime.*"

"I wouldn't push that if I were you," father said.

"While you were dancing I was wondering," August said, looking at Mrs. Bone's lipsticked mouth.

"Yes?"

"Where is your husband? Where is *Mr.* Bone?"

"August!" father said

"No, it's all right," Mrs. Bone said. "It's natural for him to be curious. Mr. Bone and I divorced about five years ago."

"Do you have children?"

"Yes, I have three daughters."

August could hardly keep from groaning. She was running true to form. He expected nothing less.

"Midgie is about your age. Deidre is younger and Thelma is older. Thelma will be going away to college next year."

August could tell she was starting to get drunk. She was on her fourth martini and was having a little trouble forming her words.

"That Deidre is the cutest little thing you ever saw!" father gushed.

"I can't wait for you to meet them," Mrs. Bone said. "Midgie is a very accomplished piano player."

August was going to ask why it was necessary for him to *ever* meet them when the waiter arrived with the food.

While he tore apart his chicken, he couldn't keep from stealing little glances at Mrs. Bone. She focused all her attention on her food as if it might disappear if she looked away. She took enormous bites, seemingly as much as her mouth would hold. Butter dribbled down her chin.

"You know," father said, wanting to be agreeable, "it does feel good to eat a meal out occasionally."

"Yes, does," Mrs. Bone said.

"The food here is excellent. I'm so glad you recommended this place."

"Um-umm," Mrs. Bone said.

When they finished eating, father and Mrs. Bone danced again. Upon returning to the table, father looked unwell. He was pale and sweating heavily. He wasn't used to whirling a bottle blonde around a dance floor and drinking hard liquor.

"I'm going to get some air," he said to Mrs. Bone.

"Do you want me to go with you?" she asked.

"No, you stay here and keep August company."

With father gone, Mrs. Bone turned to August and smiled. Her lipstick was smeared from the lobster. "So, August," she said, "tell me about yourself. What do you like to do when you're not in school?"

"I like deep-sea diving and knife throwing."

"Oh, August," she said, "you're making that up, aren't you? Your father has told me all about your over-active imagination."

"I think he's a homosexual," August said.

"Who is?"

"My father."

She looked at him and closed her eyes, exposing eyelids the color of mold. "Why would you think that?" she asked.

"He gets these mysterious phone calls at night. He goes on overnight trips and when he comes back he won't say where he's been."

"That's business. He's told me all about it."

"Sometimes when he thinks no one's looking at him, he has a secret smile on his face."

"Maybe he's just feeling happy."

"Are you going to marry him?"

"Well, I don't know. I haven't known him long enough to be thinking about that."

"I don't believe you. I think women size up men as husband material the first time they ever lay eyes on them."

She smiled indulgently, like a fond governess with a naughty child. "You're awfully worldly wise for one so young."

"Did he tell you my mother committed suicide?"

"Yes."

"Didn't it make you wonder? I mean, what reasons she might have had?"

"He said she had a chemical imbalance of the brain."

"That kind of lets him off the hook, don't you think?"

"What do you mean?"

"She hanged herself from a rafter in the attic. I found her when I came home from school that day." (August was making this up. She died in bed after washing down a half-bottle of pain pills with a fifth of whiskey. There was even some doubt if she meant to do it or if it was somehow an "accident.")

"Your father didn't tell me that."

"That's when I was eight. I've been under the care of a psychiatrist ever since."

"I'm sure it was terrible and I'm sorry for you *and* your mother."

"You see, insanity ran in her family. Not everybody in her family had it, but she had it and she passed it along to me. I have the feeling that some day I'm going to do something a *lot* worse than commit suicide. I feel it inside me waiting to come out."

"Oh."

"You probably don't want to be around when it happens."

When father came back to the table, he looked disheveled. He had loosened his tie and unbuttoned his collar. His hair, about which he was so particular, was sticking up in points.

"I'm sorry to have to break up this little party," he said, "but I'm not feeling well and I need to go home."

"Oh, dear!" Mrs. Bone said. "And it's been such a pleasant evening!"

At home, August could hear his father vomiting in the bathroom. When he came out, he looked as ill as August had ever seen him look.

"Are you all right?" August asked.

"I *will* be as soon as I get the lobster out of my system."

Later, after August had changed into his pajamas and was lying on the couch in front of the TV, his father came into the room wearing his bathrobe with nothing underneath.

"I'm going away tomorrow and will be back the next day in the evening," father said. "Will you be all right here by yourself?"

"Of course," August said.

"You won't get into any mischief?"

"No."

"What did you think of Ida?"

"What did I think of *who*?"

"Mrs. Bone. What did you think of her?"

Ida Bone, August thought. I had a bone.

"I don't want to speak ill of her," August said, "but I didn't like her."

"Why not?"

"Haven't you ever disliked anyone instinctively on sight?"

"What did you say to her when I was in the men's room being sick?'

"I didn't say anything."

"When I took her home, she was very reserved. That's not like her at all. She didn't ask me to call her as she always does and she didn't say anything about my seeing her again."

"Well, you know. Women."

"She didn't want me to kiss her goodnight."

"Ugh! Why would you want to do that?"

"I felt a definite cooling from her this evening."

"It's probably for the best," August said. "I don't think she's your type anyway."

Dear E

Byron Jones

Dear E.

By the time you read this I will be long gone. I don't mean an hour's head start, or a day, or even a week. I mean long. Perhaps one hundred years. Probably more. I have not yet made the calculation.

It's strange. It's like you are standing right behind me, leaning over my shoulder, anxious to read the next word even as I type. I feel haunted by you, yet your father's grandfather is yet to be born.

I need to tell you something. Something extremely important. Please, ignore the yellowed paper and the faded ink. This is all about where you are now, and what you are involved in at the University.

The University that has benefitted from generations of remarkably foresighted ancestors. Such ideas, what innovation, how did they do it?

The machine your students are building for you in the basement laboratory in St Michael's House is the key to the success of the Institution's founding fathers. It will deliver the greatest prize.

How the hell it works, why it does what it does no one has fathomed thus far and I don't suppose even your incredible intellectual gifts will bring us any closer to an understanding.

Whatever misgivings you might have you must trust me when I tell you that you are to turn the machine on at noon on Wednesday 17th April 2013, but do not enter the payload booth.
   I feel like I should repeat that last sentence over and over. I feel cold now. My coat is poor protection against the elements at this time of year but summer is too late to write this letter.

Put a solar powered laptop and hard drive with a copy of the contents of the University Library in the payload booth before the machine is turned on. Do not in any circumstance, enter the booth.

   I have allowed for this document to be willed through generations of Deans of College so that it arrives safely in your hands a week before the experiment. I beg God that you read it.

The machine will work in a spectacular and unexpected way. It will act on past events, but of the future I have no information. I can only warn you not to enter the payload booth.

   How and when I arrived in this God-forsaken land I do not know. But for the good people of the University, who recognised my education, I would be alone with my metal book.

Good luck,

Kindest Regards, E.

Levee Camp Moan

Eryk Pruitt

On the third night of rain, we reckoned about thirteen or so Negroes were gone. No belongings, no bodies, just gone. First thing come to mind was the river took them. After all, it'd taken everything else. But a bit of time passed now and I know better. I good and well know better, even though this is another of those stories they won't be printing in the papers down in New Orleans.

The next night seven more disappeared, and a half-dozen the night after that. Boss Mickey screamed and hollered, wanted to know what's happening to his labor, wanted to know how the hell we expected to fight this river without manpower. He wanted to know if they was running off or if they'd gotten careless around the river, got washed away. He wanted more men patrolling the levees.

"We got all the men we can spare out there already, Boss Mickey," said Gentry. He scratched at his beard which had grown out of hand. None of us had taken to appearances since the rains started coming again. "But we're stretched pretty thin now as it is."

"If we lose more Negroes," Boss Mickey said, "then we lose hold of the river. And if we lose the river, we'll lose this entire half of the state. That's your land, my land and everybody's land you hold dear so get up on that levee and make sure we lose no more Negroes."

So we rowed out there and kept watch ourselves. The sun would drop and all you heard until your ears come used to it was the river, roaring and rushing and taking whatever it wanted, taking it on down through the bluffs at Vicksburg, the hills of Natchez and into New Orleans. The light of the moon showed us where the other men stood, the levee horizon itself dotted with tiny campfires that fought against the rain to keep lit.

We walked down the levee to where the blacks now lived. More tents sprung up every day. Used to, back in the fields, this time of night would have them carrying on and singing. Every recollection I had of the sharecroppers and their cabins lent to music: their work songs, the pounding of the hammers and the chants and hollers back and forth as they labored, loved and played. Those cabins washed away after the first crevasse and no one much sang anymore. All the music was gone, leaving tents and thousands of angry refugee Negroes.

I offered one a cigarette. He spied it suspiciously but took it anyway. He stood at the edge of the camp, watching the horizon, watching river spit past and hiss. I asked him about the missing Coloreds, asked if they'd run off.

"If they's smart they did," he said. "But I don't reckon so. I reckon one of them mens up there didn't like their cut."

I looked back at the watchmen. I shook my head and told him I didn't think that was so. Boss Mickey made it clear he wanted these Negroes able to work once the waters receded, and especially if they didn't.

"You think the river took them?" I asked.

"I think there's more out there than the river's going to get us," he said.

I went to ask him what he meant by that, but the watchmen got to shooting at a dog they found rooting at the fringe of the camp. They'd issued an order to shoot dogs a week ago. Dogs roamed the camps and some had gone rabid and we'd enough fear of disease, but I'd still never get used to it. Somebody got one and sent a black fella down the embankment to roll the carcass into the current. We watched it go under, bob up, then go under a final time, never to be seen in this county again.

In some parts the levee wasn't eight feet wide. River on one side, flood on the other. Some days the river came up to the top and everyone threw sandbags from the barge on top of it, water lapping and spraying right up over them. Some days the waters receded down the sides of the levee. Folks quit any hope they used to have at the sight of the waters rolling back. The rains always came again and the sun quit rising. We'd had but dark, angry clouds since before the New Year. Instead, there were days when it got less dark and stars faded to nothing and we knew night ended.

When that night ended, three more Negroes were gone.

This time, Boss Mickey sent us back into the levee camp with a little incentive. His brother and a few boys brought their rifles and we stormed the camp around lunchtime. The Coloreds stopped loading sandbags or dirt or whatever they'd been using to fight the river as we arrived, angry and wanting answers. Men mostly, but some women stood around, wishing for something to do.

"I don't know where they's going," pleaded one of the black men. He eyeballed Boss Mickey's brother, him holding his gun and not taking eyes off the black. "If someone told me something, I'd be telling you right now, boss. You got to believe me."

"They's probably drowned," said another. "Or worse, they died eating this stuff you all's feeding us."

A few Negroes laughed, but most didn't dare. The food may not be good, but what alternative was there? Most everyone stared into the bottoms of their bean cups and kept scooping.

"We know life on the levee can be hard," said Gentry. "Trust me, we know. But we're doing everything we can to make sure your homes don't get washed out. You think that's my house down there under that water? You think its Boss Mickey's? No sir. We're all in this together to make sure you folk can go home when the water's gone."

"I ain't got nothing to go back to except money I owe sharecropping," said one of the bigger ones from Allan Hopper's land. "But ain't nobody letting us leave."

"It's a health risk," explained Gentry. "We're under orders to make sure everybody stays and helps out. If every one of you Negroes leave, then nobody will be here to help save all you people's homes."

The big Negro wanted to continue, but Boss Mickey's brother got tired of it and hit him in the face with the butt of his rifle. Big man went down and I tensed, seeing as how there were hundreds of blacks on that strip of levee and not but six of us. However, we had the guns. Nobody did nothing but weep and moan. Boss Mickey's brother didn't take to that either and came hard with the gun, but Gentry and I held him still.

"Ain't no use in busting up every one of these fellas that don't like how things are," Gentry told him. "We'd have no one left to fight the river."

I looked to the womenfolk and saw it in their eyes. They were scared. Everyone in the Delta had a right to be scared at that moment, but they weren't just scared of the river. Nor was it Boss Mickey's brother and the guns had them stretched. Something else had them. I went to talk to the one from the laundry but good Lord, thunder cracked open the sky and down came the rains again and meal time ended. Every one of us got to piling sandbags.

We worked until we heard the screaming. How long it had carried on was anyone's guess, but once we heard it, we got running. It came from the far edge on the flood side, opposite the camp and we rushed through, leaping campfires and pushing past children, rushing through half-abandoned dice games and whatnot until we reached the edge of the levee. Our eyes, slow to adjust to darkness, saw nothing. More Negroes heard the scream and gathered behind us to see what caused the ruckus but nobody stepped past Gentry or I, as if to protect them from what may or may not be there.

"Do you see it?" Gentry demanded. I held up my hand to listen but heard nothing but save floodwaters lapping against the levee. No one moved. I held my breath. Beech leaves rattled like bones. Then, after a moment, we heard sounds of visceral tearing and chewing. I squinted and made out a dark silhouette crouched at the side of the levee and called out to it. It froze. The sound stopped. What light we had was scant and I saw no more than its outline and two yellowed eyes. I called again and whatever it was turned to us and hissed, then leapt into the waters and was gone.

"What the hell was that?" Gentry cried. He ran to the waterside and stepped in to his ankles. "Did you see that?"

I told him yes, I saw it, but I couldn't describe or know what it was. All I saw in my mind were those yellowed eyes.

"Was it human?"

It looked human.

The negroes backed away, wanting nothing to do with this. Gentry sloshed in the water, still looking for answers and suddenly he was down, flailing in the muddy overflow. I clung tight to my rifle but rushed down the levee to retrieve him should he be carried away by the current or worse, but he regained composure and rose to the banks.

"What the hell?" He dragged something to the shore. I wiped rain from my eyes. It was a negro, one of the bigger ones, and he'd been half-eaten.

The camp erupted with the discovery. Many negroes didn't care who had guns and who would used them or even if they would, they gathered what little they still owned and loaded onto the barge. Boss Mickey himself appeared at the levee and demanded the captains remove them and depart for Vicksburg, but more piled on.

"You didn't see what George and I saw," Gentry insisted.

"I don't think you and George saw what you think you saw," said Boss Mickey. "What I see is my men standing by while the entire Delta labor force tries to escape. If I have to sink that barge I will, but I will not watch these people quit their duties. Now get them off that barge!"

We did and that night lost four more and the next day they wouldn't work. Boss Mickey's brother brought his scattergun and pointed it this way and that but no one budged. They weren't loading sandbags.

"What's the point, boss?" asked the one from Allan Hopper's place. "They's something out there eating colored folk and if we fight the river, we'll live to feed it. I'd rather the river take us."

Boss Mickey's brother listened to the reasoning then decided he didn't like it so he pointed his scattergun into the negro's face and fired. The front of his head exploded into a fine, red mist that took with it all the pain and fear he'd felt since the rains come and the rest of him fell to the flood side. Boss Mickey's brother stepped over the body and considered it a bit while the blacks screamed and protested and pitched a fit then choked up as the white man kicked the body into the muddy waters.

"Who else don't want to haul sandbags today?" he asked and in no time, they were back to work.

Someone proposed all this rain was on account of something someone did, as if an irritant to a cranky God, so folks set to praying even more. Others said it could be disease, that a worker got bit by one of the dogs gone rabid or ate something bad or maybe the typhus finally arrived, so a few Red Cross boys made their way from downriver in a motor boat with vaccine. Boss Mickey's brother and his men rounded coloreds at gunpoint and lined them up for immunizations and we figured that would be that, but six more went missing that night and once more the camp was in a panic the next morning when the sun didn't come up.

Boss Mickey had enough. He decided we'd wasted too many resources fiddling with this river and our worries and the pressure on our earthworks could both be eased by dynamiting the levee on the other side. Flooding the town on the other side would save our own and he had no time for ghost stories coming out of negro camps. The levee could go any day if we didn't act fast. He left that job to Gentry and I.

We readied for night. The rains, as if to conspire with Boss Mickey for our deadly mission, ceased. The current swept stronger than an angry sea, so we took two of the strongest blacks for the rowing. We sat along the riverside and looked to the opposite banks, now further than I'd ever remembered them being. Before, we'd traded with folk from over yonder, now we were tasked with putting them underwater.

"Let's go," whispered Gentry. The negroes put oars to water and we set course for the other side.

We fought from the onset. This current moved houses, motor cars, dead and bloated mules and livestock at a steady clip and would not idle as we tried to cross. A good half hour of rowing put us no more than a quarter mile from the banks where we'd started. Our negroes tired, so we fastened our craft to a sycamore that once stood mighty and tall but now only the treetop peeked above the waterline. The blacks collapsed to the bottom of the boat and their lungs pleaded for respite. On the levee behind us, I saw orange dots from lanterns and the tiny glow of campfires, but heard little over the raging current, as if watching a moving picture show. I thought to myself that if we just untied our craft from the top of this sycamore and stayed upright and true, we'd make Vicksburg in an hour and never needed look back.

But that thought never came to words as one of the negroes protested and bucked, threw all his weight against the side of the boat and groaned violently. I raised my rifle to stop him from throwing us overboard, but froze. Someone came over the side of the boat and grabbed hold of the negro and wasn't letting go. His companion scattered and cowered behind Gentry and I who held fast, screaming and hollering. The attacker grasped the negro quick and sunk his teeth into his neck while he screamed then made no other sound as he was pulled over the side and suddenly it was as if nothing had ever happened, as if he never existed, as if the whole affair were but a dream.

The remaining negro carried on until told to shut it.

"How the hell did he get here?" asked Gentry. "Climb the tree? He didn't swim against that current. Impossible! Did you get a good look at him?"

I did, but I didn't want to say what I saw. I'd seen a man eat another, then pull him overboard. I'd seen those yellowed eyes, just like the other thing we'd seen. But I didn't want to talk about that, for the river grew in size. It had been growing for months, but now with three of us alone in the tiny rowboat offshore in the dark, it became an ocean. Alone? We only hoped so. Our mission tasked us to keep rowing, but I wanted no more to do with this water, this river. I wanted out of the boat. I wanted to run.

I heard splashing on the stern side and not just catfish jumping or the last struggles of cattle flushing downriver, but splashing as if swimming and fired my rifle in its direction.

"What are you doing?" Gentry screamed.

More splashing, but this time on the starboard side and I fired my gun and figured we were all in for it. I ordered the negro to row us back to shore, but he couldn't be pulled from the bottom of the skiff. I picked up the oar and slapped at the water, told Gentry to keep guns at the ready. We were still tied to the sycamore and I screamed and pleaded with the negro to quit cowering, to unfasten us, but to no use. Gentry fired his rifle twice in different directions into the night, but still the thrashing and splashing against the current and I dropped the oar and pulled at the rope binding us to the tree.

"What the hell is happening on the levee?" Gentry cried. I shook loose the knot, turned and saw. The orange lantern lights flew like fireflies. Silhouettes darted to and fro before the campfire's glow, sparking embers as people were thrown into them. At first I thought Boss Mickey's brother had stormed the place, but I knew better. Over the current I heard shouts and screams and knew that what had taken the negroes had returned and would take more. They were being overrun.

Gentry fired onto the levee. I pushed free of the sycamore and let the skiff fall into the current. The weeping negro in the bottom of the boat covered his eyes. We sailed past the levee camp, too fast to see everything, but we saw enough. We saw Boss Mickey's brother would shoot no more negroes. We saw no one would take issue with the food anymore. We saw no one would be there to fight the river or defend the levee any longer, which had to be a good thing, because I swore if the river didn't swallow that camp, Gentry and I would return with the dynamite, if we dared come back at all.

The Bleeding Tree

Jennifer Jones

"Don't touch that," she said.

"Why?" The child asked.

"You know why," she answered.

"Because it's the bleeding tree?" The child pressed.

"Yes."

"Does it have blood in it?"

"Yes."

"Will it get blood on me?"

"Probably." The woman paused before lifting her gaze from the basket in front of her. "Keep working."

The child sighed. "But everything's dead."

"I know," the woman said, dropping another fistful of brown muck into the basket. "We're-"

"Clearing it for the next planting, I know, I know," The child said, index finger dancing across the mud to create a family of stick figures. "But it's always dead. Nothing ever grows."

"We still have to do it."

"Why?"

"Because she tells us to," the woman answered.

"Do we always got to do what she says?"

"Yes."

"Why?" The child asked.

"She gives us a room."

The child fisted her hand in the mud, watching as it jetted between her fingers. Over them, the bleeding tree loomed, one branch stretched out wide as if to wrap them in an embrace. "Is my dad in the bleeding tree?"

"Yes."

"Why?" The child asked.

"You know why," she answered.

"Because he put me in your tummy?"

"Yes."

"Without asking?"

"Yes."

"So, if I poke the tree will his blood come out?"

"Yes," she answered.

"I thought people hanged on the tree, though. Miss Ida called it the hanging tree," the child said.

"So?" The woman asked.

"Why do you call it the bleeding tree?"

"Because all death is blood."

"Oh," the child said.

"And don't talk to Miss Ida."

"Why?"

"Because I told you not to, child," she answered.

"Why is she sad all the time, Mommy?" The child asked.

"Because her husband is gone," she said.

"Where'd he go?"

"He's in the bleeding tree."

"With my Daddy?" The child asked.

The woman hesitated. "Yes."

The old porch groaned under Miss Ida's weight as she opened the creaking door and stepped out onto the threshold. She was a crone draped in black wool; narrowed, milky black eyes flitted around the garden. Mother said Miss Ida was going blind. The old woman's eyes were drawn to the shadowy silhouette of the bleeding tree and her lips began to move, chant. Spit pooled at the corner of her mouth then slid in a glob down her chin. The woman stood and took the child's hand. "Come, today is not a good day," she said and the child was ushered inside the house.

That night the child went to sleep, listening to the bleeding tree scratch messages into her window, and in the morning, Miss Ida was back normal. She was dressed pristinely, as usual, her hair done up in a tight bun, and jewels around her neck. She was completely out of place in the decaying home. The woman gripped the child's shoulder as Miss Ida swept gracefully out onto the porch. "You must stay inside today," she said.

"Why?"

"Because we're going to feed the bleeding tree," she answered.

"Oh," the child said, "who?"

"Mrs. Douglas."

"What'd she do?" The child asked.

The women knelt beside her, combing her fingers through the child's messy hair. "Do you remember when Kitty had her first kittens? And she was scared because she never had any kittens before and-"

"And she gobbled them all up!" The child exclaimed.

"Sometimes mommies do that to." The woman said.

"Oh…" the child paused, "Mama?"

"What, child?"

"I'm glad you didn't gobble me up," the child said.

The woman didn't answer.

For The Love Of Books

Diya Gangopadhyay

This is the evening Dharini has been looking forward to for months now. Or more specifically, the brown envelope that has been awaiting her in the mailbox this evening when she got back from school. The last part of her favorite novel "The Blue Sky", which was released and shipped to her today. She ran to the attic holding her breath, eager to discover how her year long journey with this novel, something that permeated into and completely engulfed the reality she lived in, would culminate.

She had hardly realized when this apparently fictitious narrative became so much a part of her being. And its protagonist Indira her living companion. The closest companion she has had in the fifteen years of her life. So much so that her immediate surroundings and its people seemed alien at times. She had seen Indira growing up, evolving through the pages of her favorite book, from a young girl full of dreams born to the most culturally influential family in a fictitious city to a brave-heart ready to fight the world.

The book had gripped her from the very first pages. The imagined reality of this family comprising prominent literary figures, the cult like influence they had on the psyche of their hometown, ruling them by the might of the pen, all seemed like utopia. This family was home to her fantasy friend Indira, growing up listening in awe to some of the brightest minds discussing poetry, rhetoric and ideas in her living room. She woke up to lines from Shakespeare and recited Wordsworth. At bedtime, her mother read to her excerpts from books written by her father as well as her own verses. She listened into writers' debates and beamed with pride when book-lovers across the nation swore by her parents' and grandfathers' books. Why couldn't real life be like that, Dharini wondered. Why did she have to bother with the mundane rituals of existence that always had a way of interrupting her reverie? Why were her parents so concerned about her seeming disconnectedness with her "real surroundings" and her friends perplexed that she found an imaginary person more enchanting than tangible pleasures?

Life progressed in days and in pages of the book. Life that happened in the school bus rides, long nights in the quiet room in the attic, sneaked in bits of time between classes, lunch breaks, and even the dinner table. Indira grew up bit by bit; Indira who articulated her deepest thoughts in words so beautiful that Dharini could only marvel at them, Indira who despite being surrounded by others' thoughts and opinions had a view of her own, (and how pristine everything was when seen with her eyes!); Indira who was the treasure of this great enlightened family and the one to carry the baton; Indira who had the life Dharini dreamed to have.

It was in the second part of the book that imperfections started to creep into the blissful life of Indira. Complexities that made it all the more intriguing. Indira, a little older and wiser now, started to notice that the living room conferences were not quite the forum for free thought that she had so far believed them to be. That her family was not quite the selfless patrons of blossoming talent and unbiased critics that they projected themselves to be. Indira's gradual disillusionment had conflicting effects on Dharini. At one level an erstwhile perfect world was crumbling. At another level, the person through whose eyes she saw this world was becoming even more enchanting. The way Indira's belief was shaken by little things; her father deriding a young writer who criticized one of his works, even though Indira thought his critique to be valid; her elder brother ridiculing a manuscript which she thought was refreshingly different, and a few such other incidents. Indira began to observe that there was indeed a pattern in the kind of writing her family upheld and the kind they looked down upon. That the kind of work they patronized had semblances of their own genre, the same grandiose language, the lofty spiritual themes as opposed to the earthiness and everyday life focus of this other variety. Her budding mind was in a dilemma for a while, "Is there only one kind of good writing?" she asked herself. Hadn't she been told right since childhood that if she could relate so deeply to a piece of writing and be stimulated by it, then it is valuable irrespective of what style and genre it is? Why then were her elders acting in an apparently contradictory manner?

Dharini read, engrossed. She was being posed with questions that had never occurred to her before, that made her stop and ponder for hours, much like her counterpart in the book. She thought as Indira thought and along with her came to the same conclusion, that different, contrasting themes and styles could be equally beautiful. That it is their co-existence that made the world of books more captivating. She was surprised at how her own thinking was evolving to be so much like Indira's, floating through similar waves of doubts, questions, rationale, and finally landing at the same place.

There came a day when Indira realized that her family who owned a publishing house and had tremendous influence over the other major publishers in the town, made a deliberate effort to ensure that the work of this "other" breed of writers never saw the light of day. It took her a long time to believe that discrimination could go to this extent. That the same people who had taught her to open up her mind to diversity would indulge in an act of this nature. The more Indira thought about this dichotomy, the clearer she was that this was not something she would watch from the sidelines. That if she had to choose between defying what she believed and the people who shaped those beliefs it had to be the latter.

It was life changing for Dharini as well. It made Dharini wonder as to how much of what she believed, was asked to believe to be sacrosanct in her own life actually held ground. She began to ponder upon and question everything she was told, made it a point to try and view things from Indira' perspective, base her thoughts and actions on what Indira would think of it had she been there for real. At times she felt like there stood a wall between her and her surroundings. That everything around was far away and the pages of this book were the only tangible thing.

Towards the end of the second part, Indira became an instrument of the change she wished to bring about. As a budding writer herself, though she was yet to formally publish a book, she had quite a following for her own online diary where she poured her thoughts unbridled. It was the only space she could call her own, where she was known as herself and not as the daughter of the grand family she belonged to. Dharini could relate to this yearning for freedom, for a voice of her own. A yearning for being considered not for who she was and the people she was related to, but for her own mind and ideas. It inspired her to take to writing as well. So one fine day when Indira had a chance meeting with one of the many writers to whom her family had denied publishing rights owing to "a below par and unimaginative style", she asked for the draft of the book. How radically different it was from all that she had been growing up reading! None of the floaty floweriness, none of the larger than life surrealism. Instead what she found was very conversation like description of everyday lives. Stories of people who were extraordinary in their ordinariness. It was a glimpse into a world that Indira only had a vague notion of so far. It infuriated her to think that it would reach no one else and fade into oblivion. She failed to understand why her family would resent against such writing. Did they sense a threat in the emerging trend of an alternative, down-to-earth style of writing focusing on seemingly banal occurrences which was so starkly different from their own work? Was there a sense of insecurity that propelled such unfathomable discrimination against something new?

Indira confronted everyone in her family about this. "How can it be that you do not find it worth being read by all? Does its simplicity and true to life nature of the writing not appeal to you?" she asked everyone at home. "Aren't these qualities you always treasured and praised?" Only to be told that they had "responsibilities for shaping up the tastes of the masses and could not let sub-standard work go out into the world". They even told Indira that she was young and her sensibilities not "refined enough to tell wheat from chaff". Indira quit arguing and instead thought of an alternative route. She decided to feature one such unpublished story each day in her own online magazine, the one place where she was not controlled by anyone. It soon became a movement popular and widespread enough for her father to take notice of her blatant disobedience.

And for Dharini to be completely smitten, and swear by the courage of her role model of the book world. For so many days now she had felt that her own real life was lived by rules made by others; parents, teachers, peers, et al. That she was rewarded for living by a set protocol. Indira's rebellion appealed to a dormant yearning in her to break free, to do something that only she believed in despite what everyone else thought of it. Except that Indira had found a purpose to break free, and Dharini sought hers vicariously in the pages of this book. Through Indira, Dharini experienced what it is like to be a positive change to the lives of so many writers, to be their channel of expression, to be a hero, leader with a following, at a growing age. Dharini would imagine herself becoming a little bit of Indira in her own life, standing up for a reason and bringing about a change she wished to see.

In the days leading to the release of the third and final part of the novel, Dharini had sketched out all possible ways in which the story could end. Perhaps Indira would use her fiery words to actually change the minds of all the elders in the family? Perhaps the popularity of her online movement would make them realize that something that so resonated with the people could not be kept in the shelves? Or maybe like a classical heroine Indira would leave home and be one with the people she led? Dharini was not sure which of the endings she liked the most or which one was the likeliest. Sometimes she liked one, and at other times she preferred another. She even began to jot down dialogues she would like to see her role-model mouth.

And today was the day she would get her answers, she had the final part of the book in her hand. Of course dinner was impossible to attend to. Her friends, who came over to invite her for a meetup, relented when they saw her with the book. She had to be left alone in her own world today. Nothing else could matter.

But what was this? The novel did not culminate in any of the ways Dharini had envisioned it. At the end of it, she began to feel this was not the Indira she had known so well all these days. Where was her heroic spark and unabated courage? In the course of the conflict described in this part of the novel between her and the others in her family, Indira did not for once try to convince the elders of what she thought to be right. Rather, her entire belief system was stirred and she decided that she had a lot more to learn than what her comfortable home would allow her to. The novel ended with Indira, full of doubt and questions, leaving home to explore the world, travel, meet people beyond her immediate realm and and re-assess all that she has believed so far, with a fresh perspective.

To Dharini, it was massively disappointing, almost defeatist. How could Indira doubt herself when she had always been so right? Why did she not have the strength to stand up for her beliefs? She began to question if she actually knew her best friend and constant companion of the past one year at all. She asked all the people around her. Of course answers like "It is a story after all" and "It was the author's vision" did not suffice. For all these days, in every situation of her life Dharini had wondered what Indira would think if she happened to be here. Indira was the voice of wisdom in her life, her friend, philosopher and guide. How could that person be unsure of herself, and say that she needed to evolve and grow before she could firmly believe in anything?

After weeks of restless wondering, Dharini's father pointed out to something that seemed like a shimmer of hope. "Look girl, the author of your obsession, Dr. Srinivas is coming to Crossword this Saturday." Dharini listened with keenness. "He will be reading out excerpts from his novel and be taking questions. So here's your chance." How fascinating! She would finally get to meet the person who created Indira. Didn't some of the reviews also say the novel bore hints of an autobiography? Here's the path to all her unanswered questions. However, the answers she had hoped for were not to come. When she met Dr. Srinivas, his vision of Indira seemed so different from the person in Dharini's mind. For him, Indira was never the firm heroine who always knew what is right, but rather a growing girl whose views and beliefs were constantly changing. For whom, the conflict between what she had been told since childhood and her own intuitions grew to be so large that she did not know what to believe. And was compelled to go out and figure things out for herself.

Dharini came back disillusioned that night. By now the questions in her mind were losing their fervor. She was almost ready to reconcile to a realization that she had indeed been fascinated by someone she hardly understood. And even the simple fact that it was after all a character in a book written by someone else.

The next morning though, Dharini woke up to a rather surprising e-mail from Dr Srinivas. She opened it half-heartedly, not quite looking forward to more disillusionment. But surprisingly, what the e-mail had to say soothed her weeks of restlessness and gave it a whole new meaning!

It said, "Dear Dharini, I am indeed overwhelmed that my book has had such a deep influence on a bright young mind like you. The way you have been living the reality of this book is indeed an author's dream come true. As writers we envision characters and situations from our own experiences of the world and our imaginations. But they gain completeness only with what readers like you build out of them. By themselves they are page-full of words. It is the reader who accords them with existence, bringing them into their own lives and realities. It is heartening that in your imaginative mind, Indira has become a person quite different from the one I had originally thought her to be. Your Indira is indeed as real as mine. Do not be disturbed if your interpretation does not coincide with the author's vision. A book is as much a product of your imagination as you read it as it is the author's. Best wishes."

Dharini knew what she wanted to do next. She would pull up the notebook where she had once jotted down the possible endings to her favorite book and flesh out her favorite one – just as a whimsical act of exploration – the one that matches her notion of Indira. After all who says a book cannot have many alternate endings?

Sports Bar Conversation, Overheard

Bob Carlton

Oh, hey...check out the TV.

Wow, John, that's fascinating. Sweden versus South Korea. Nothing like a little women's World Cup qualifying...

No, no Buck. The TV above the bar...What's that?...Yeah, another round. Put it on his tab.

Hey! Are you talking about me? What did you say?

Nothing Buck. Just go back to women's soccer.

So, what are we looking at John?

Isn't that the Vergiss trial, Sybil?

So, yeah I think so.

Well, you guys know what it's all about, right?

So, isn't that the girl that killed her best friend, like, over something really dumb?

Yeah, she got forty years or something.

Then what is all this about?

You didn't hear, Nikki? Oh, this is freaking brilliant. Amy Vergiss' mom is suing the Lifetime Channel, or whoever owns it, maybe even some production company, God knows who all else who may be connected, for that movie, *Primal Curse.*

So, I saw that.

Jesus Sybil, you know watching Lifetime gives all women a bad name.

So no, Nikki, it was really good. Based on that short story by, oh, what's-his-name?

"All May Be Well" by Bram Chastain.

So yeah, we had to read that for Dr. Carrington's class last semester.

All of you were in that class, right?

So, I know Nikki and I were. Hey Buck, were you in Carrington's Con. Lit. class last semester?

Hey! What was that crap? Yeah, I better see a yellow card!

Anyway, to get back to the point of all this. I guess it's just a weird coincidence, because I'm...Buck, give this woman a five...oh no, thank *you*...Anyway, I've based my Senior Project on that story. Hang on, I got all that stuff in here somewhere.

Goal!

Here we go. Well, first, you guys know about Carrington and Chastain, right?

Well, duh...Bram Chastain is only the most famous graduate this university ever had.

Right Nik, and Carrington was like his mentor. And of course, Chastain is one of those reclusive types that is no help to academics who pick apart his work, which is kind of an advantage, because he's not going to say you're right or wrong, one way or the other. But, Carrington knows his stuff inside and out, so I got some first rate insight to get me started.

What's your project about?

Well, through a little research and some dumb luck, I've stumbled on the source of Chastain's story.

So, you mean like he stole it?

No, no Sybil. Think of it as like his inspiration. It gave him the germ of an idea. I mean, if you read this magazine article and then the story, you might think, well, there are some echoes maybe, but the two stories are totally different. But the cool thing is, once you start digging around, there are all sorts of little clues that pretty much clinch it.

Then your Senior Project is basically showing how some magazine article is the source of the Bram Chastain story, "All May Be Well." That about got it?

That, Nikki in a nutshell, is it.

Well then, my question would be: who cares? I mean, maybe not who cares, but, why does it really matter?

Excellent question, N., one which I myself have wrestled with long into the night. I have two answers for you, one cynical, one aesthetic. The cynical answer is that it only matters as a kind of academic finger exercise, the kind of mental masturbation that ivory tower careers are founded on. The aesthetic answer is that this is kind of a window into how one guy's mind operates. You see the creative process at ground level. What details does he keep, and why? What does it tell you about what he thinks writing is all about? I know it all sounds a little obscure, and maybe absurd or stupid, but once you get into it, it can get really fascinating.

So, check it out. Is that Amy Vergiss?

Yeah, I think that's footage from the actual murder trial.

Hey, Johnny dude! Man, that chick is hot!

Good Lord, Buck, what are you talking about? She's like eighty pounds overweight, and that jailhouse haircut isn't exactly helping with the whole slimming problem.

Man, you're nuts. Picture the hair not tied in a ponytail.

Buck, what are you talking about?

The Swedish goaltender, dude; what are you talking about?

The Amy Vergiss trial.

Oh man, she's a pig!

Nice Buck, very nice. Waitress...another round please, put it on his tab.

What? hey, are you all talking about me again?

Go back to sleep Buck. So where was I?

The great detective had found the smoking gun.

Oh yeah, here we go. Through a long series of brilliant missteps, which I won't go into right now, I came across this: an article in *Texas Monthly*, from July 1996, by one Skip Hollandsworth.

Oh come on, is that even a real name?

Yes, Nikki my love, it is. "Poisoning Daddy" by Skip Hollandsworth.

And this is the inspiration for "All May Be Well"?

Absolutely N. As my grandfolks would say, dig this. In 1993, a high school girl in Texas poisoned her dad. It was the perfect murder, but guilt eventually overtakes her and she confesses. In "All May Be Well", an eight year old girl kills her little sister. No one suspects foul play, until ten years later, guilt overtakes her and she confesses.

So, but John, in the Lifetime movie, the girl kills her brother.

True enough, Syb, but I think they did that for dramatic, or really melodramatic, effect. Now, I must confess that I have seen *Primal Curse...*

Really? You, oh Lord of the Highbrow?

Due diligence, N., due diligence.

So, what do you mean, dramatic effect?

Well, Syb, I think they changed it so you could get that whole dad-wracked-with-grief-at-the-death-of-his-only-son thing. They really play up the dad's guilt, him thinking he didn't have the baby gate up right, thinking he should have been paying more attention, and so forth.

Then you can get the inevitable descent into depression, alcoholism, and finally suicide. It's so over the top it's idiotic.

So, well then, why do it if it wasn't in the story?

I'll take this one, John. See Sybil, when you write a story, half the point of it is in the way you tell it. You can get away with a lot less action, because since it all exists only in language, the reader is filling in blanks along the way, creating the story in her own mind from the images and words on the page.

Yeah, something like that. See, with a movie, especially a movie geared toward a Lifetime audience, you have a passive viewer. It's like a lot of genre fiction, too, actually; reading a lot of that stuff is really no more than watching a movie. The whole point is to reinforce the viewer's expectations, not challenge them. They're just watching, waiting to be entertained, so you have to wipe out all the nuance and leave them with a nice juicy plot to keep their butts planted on the couch and their brains in neutral, all blank and receptive to whatever tampon or douche producer is buying up commercial time to plant the seeds of artificial need...

Alright, John, enough already...

Sorry Nikki, I digress. I will merely give one example of what I mean. In the movie, the scene when the murder takes place, it's just the girl looking all angry and jealous-like, at the little boy, who is sitting at the baby gate whining. It's like the baby is just pissing the girl off with his noise. So the next thing you see is Dad downstairs, on the couch, watching TV, not minding the kids. Then you hear a crash and something tumbling down the stairs. You hear the girl yell "Daddy!". Then the scene cuts to a close-up of her face, staring blank and stony into the camera for a few seconds, before she turns and walks away. It's just so conventional and predictable. Chastain has it this way: "One day, the two children were alone upstairs, and at one point found themselves near the baby gate that blocked off the staircase. Dorothy, watching her baby sister playing quietly by the gate with a doll that had once been Dorothy's, saw her opportunity and took it." It's all so understated; no histrionics, no noise, no dad explicitly being negligent. And I love that detail, the doll, once Dorothy's, symbolic of the little sister's usurpation.

Wow, John, usurpation? Can we get back to the matter at hand now?

OK. Now, this girl in Texas, her name was Marie Robards. Her best friend says about her, "Marie is, like, *gorgeous*! In high school she was one of the most mature girls I had ever met. I thought, 'Wow, if I hang around her, she'll keep me motivated, help me act a little more serious.'" Then a little further down it says, "She was an excellent student, reserved but polite, the kind of girl who never acted impulsively, never stayed out too late or had too much to drink at parties." Her father's girlfriend at the time said, "In all honesty, she was what you wanted a teenager to be." Then, after the murder, she goes to a new school. I quote: "At Mansfield High School, Marie was known as a straight-A type. She joined the volleyball

90

team and the yearbook staff." And, et cetera et cetera, quoting a teacher here: "[S]he had this hunger to get involved. When we had our University Interscholastic League competitions, Marie was interested in everything—drama, journalism, and keyboarding." Now, compare all that with the way Chastain opens: "For the last ten years, Dorothy Jason had lived what most of her peers would perceive as a blessed life, and what most of their parents would see as an exemplary one. She excelled in whatever endeavor she undertook, and she undertook a great many. She was a straight-A student, captain of the debate and softball teams, and an accomplished actress in theater."

Interesting John, but not exactly beyond the realm of coincidence.

Oh man! Just missed!

Wow...is Buck even with us anymore? Anyway, Nik...

Wait, what? Are you talking about me again?

Sorry Buck, go back to metaphorical sleep. Oh, and as long as I have your attention, order another round will you? It's your turn to buy. Anyway, there's a lot more than that. For instance, after Marie Robards killed her dad, she ends up staying, oddly enough, with her paternal grandfather. In explanation, we get this from her mom: "I think Marie somehow wanted to make up to the Robards family and be the best granddaughter there was. She was determined to start a new life." Chastain puts it this way: "To many in the community, it seemed that perhaps

Dorothy was driven by a need for recognition and approval, a need. They believed, at least partially in reaction to the death of her little sister, whose memory seemed to be a shadow out of which Dorothy was attempting to emerge. To all appearances, she had worked to help her parents through their grief, working to achieve in a single life what might have been done in two." This is followed, of course, by the big disclosure: "Dorothy had indeed dedicated her life to escaping what for her was more ghost than shadow, a memory to obliterate rather than honor, for unbeknownst to those who lauded her dedication and drive all these years, Dorothy Jason was intent on forgetting that it was she who had murdered her sister."

Powerful stuff indeed, John, but that one seems a bit of a stretch.

Well, there are other examples in the article, of her trying to leave the past behind, start over, all that. She never talks about her past, there are different versions remembered by different students concerning her dad's whereabouts, she tells her best friend she doesn't even know where her dad's grave is. It seems obvious to me there is this tension between trying to forget the past and make up for it at the same time. Like in Chastain, where you get this passage: "Even as she strove to forget, her guilt expanded as her moral sense expanded. It was as if she felt the need to earn the right to her own life, to somehow prove to the world that she could make up for whatever was lost with Penny's death."

I don't know John that one sounds a little thin to me. Sure

you're not reading into the article what you found in the story? A sort of literary reverse engineering?

Nikki, Nikki, Nikki. Even if that were the case, you think I wouldn't have more? I'm saving the best for last, so you can get acclimatized to the slow unfolding of my genius.

So, how many have you had?

Why Syllable, I'm insulated. Now listen up, and prepare to be amazed. First things first: the revelation of guilt. In the *TM* article, we have Marie's best friend quoting from *Hamlet:* "In her most dramatic voice—which was only slightly affected by her Texas drawl—Stacey recited Claudius' agonizing speech in which he wonders if he can ever repent: 'My fault is past. But oh, what form of prayer / Can serve my turn? "Forgive me my foul murder?" / That cannot be, since I am still possessed / Of those effects for which I did the murder...' 'Isn't that cool!' Stacey said. But when she looked across the table, Marie had turned pale and her hands were trembling. 'Stacey,' Marie asked, 'do you think people can go through life without a conscience?' Stacey answered, 'Well, how about the kind of person who can look somebody in the eye and kill him in cold blood?'" Marie then bursts into tears and confesses what she's done. Now, in Chastain, he changes the way it comes out, but the basic device is the same. Quote: "Dorothy's guilt would wait in mute rage, until, after ten years of silence, a senior English class would set it loose upon her in all its fury. 'Turn to page forty-seven,' Mr. Canton told his largely bored and uninterested students, '"The Tell-Tale Heart" by Edgar Allan Poe. Dorothy, would you please start for us.' She began with her customary fluidity of expression. However, her voice began to falter and crack as she made her way through the first paragraph. '" Object there was none. Passion there was none. I loved the old man. He had never wronged me. He had never given me insult."' As her voice trailed off, she slipped from her desk and down onto her knees on the floor. 'Dorothy, are you alright?' asked Mr. Canton, as a collective, puzzled silence settled over the class. In a daze, Dorothy began to speak, 'The old man...didn't really do any--...deserve to...she...he was innocent.'" There is, of course, the obligatory trip to the school nurse, assumptions of stress and overextending herself by teachers and parents, rumors of abuse or pregnancy by peers, and so on. Amidst all the various speculations and such, Dorothy confides in her best friend, Isabella Stoner: "'I can't do it anymore Izzy, I just can't.' 'What's the matter Dottie? It's not true, that stuff Libby and them are saying about you?'" I might add the editorial aside here that Libby is the name of Marie Robards' best friend's mom. To continue, quoting Dorothy: "'I wish it were Izzy.' 'Don't say that,' Isabella replied, unable just then to fathom what could possibly be worse than the rumors then circulating. Dorothy burst into tears, covering her face with her hands as she sobbed out the words Isabella was sure she could not have heard correctly, 'I murdered my own sister.' 'What?' Dorothy wiped her face with the back of her left hand, then folded both hands in her lap, straightened up in her chair, and spoke clearly, 'I killed my little sister.' 'I didn't even know you had a sister,' Isabella replied, still not quite able to take this confession in its entirety."

So, wait. Chastain changes *Hamlet* into "The Tell-Tale

Heart". Didn't *Primal Curse* change it back to *Hamlet*?

Exactly, Syllabus. Wait a second, let me find my notes on the movie.

Wow, you didn't just watch this movie, you really *watched* this movie.

You mock me Nicholas? As I said before, due diligence. At any rate, yeah, here it is. In the movie, Dorothy is called on in class to recite from the same passage that's quoted in *Texas Monthly,* except that it's taken from the beginning of Claudius' soliloquy, Act III, Scene III: "O, my offence is rank, it smells to heaven; It hath the primal eldest curse upon it,--a brother's murder!" What's weird is, I don't think any of the screenwriters would have been aware of the Robards case. I mean, it's a movie based on a five year old story that itself is based on a twenty year old magazine article. So why the change? I don't know. Maybe the brother's murder rang a bell. Or one of them recognized the reference in the title of the story. "All May Be Well"--those are Claudius' closing words in that little speech. So Hollandsworth quotes the friend quoting Claudius, from which speech Chastain apparently got his title, from which speech the writers of *Primal Curse* extract their confession.

So, that's all pretty neat, but I'm not sure it helps make your case.

Quite right. I just think it's a strange series of facts. Now, let's consider the endings of our twin, conjoined if you will, stories. In the article, Hollandsworth quotes the psychologist hired by Marie's lawyers when he visits her in jail: "Marie asked me if she could get her college degree while she was in prison. She told me she was anxious to start some kind of schooling, to improve herself, to accept her punishment and move on. She was wearing these paper clothes, which the jailers give prisoners on suicide watch, and she was shivering in her cold jail cell. But she told me she had no right to complain about her own problems because she had already cause so much suffering. It was sort of amazing to listen to her." Now of course Chastain, in true postmodern fashion, leaves his story open-ended on the question of whether or not Dorothy is convicted, let alone sent to prison. I mean, the implication is that getting a grand jury indictment under the circumstances was enough to render a verdict and dispense justice in the court of public opinion. Dorothy's life, as she had known it up to that point, is over. So she's left, twisting in the wind, making her final speech: "I can never go back. My mom, my dad—I can never face them again. But I can't complain. I did this to myself. There is no one else to blame. All I can do is try and start over. Again." And of course, all that leads us to question the title: is it ironic, or does it hold out hope? The one thing I do know is, Chastain's not saying.

Geez John, you're starting to sound like Dr. Carrington.

So, let's hear some more. I mean, all your stuff so far sounds good, but...

Oh ye of little faith. OK, so much for textual parallels. Alright, I assume Dr. Carrington went into some of

Chastain's tendencies toward sub textual, inter textual, meta textual goofiness?

Yeah, but I don't think he quite put it that way.

Well, that's where the real meat of the argument lies. For example, I already mentioned the title; that's one. Even though *Hamlet* becomes "The Tell-Tale Heart", he refers back to *Hamlet*. That by itself may be coincidence, but how about this: why "The Tell-Tale Heart"?

I don't know, seems like a fairly obvious substitution.

Consider this: the prosecutor in the Robards case was Mitch Poe. Now, even if we think of that as a possible coincidence, consider this: the co-prosecutor's name was Fred Rabalais, Jr. So the DA in Chastain, what is his name? Fred Mitchell, Jr.

Alright, now I admit it sounds like you have something there.

Wait, it gets better. Dr. Carrington pointed this one out to me. Look at Mitchell's speech to the grand jury near the end: "When a person is born free, never has to worry about where his next meal is coming from, and keeps good company, well, that person has a natural inclination toward virtue. But it's also in a person's nature to want what's forbidden, to desire what's denied. But what or when was it that Dorothy Jason was ever denied?" And it goes on from there, concerning the whole egocentric, attention-grabbing, neediness theme, but the important thing is that Dr. Carrington spotted that passage as being

pretty much straight out of Rabelais. See, Rabelais-
Rabalais?

So weird.

Right. And for Dr. Carrington it was kind of problematic,
it didn't have any real reason to be there, it could have
been Plato or Pol Pot, it didn't matter. But see, now it
does. Chastain's making a reference to his source.

That is pretty good. So let's hear more genius revealed.

Come on, come on! Sven-*ya!* Sven-*ya!* Sven-*ya!* Goal!

Well, okay, here is one final little nugget for you. Consider
our heroine's name: Dorothy Jason. According to this
article, Marie Robards' full given name was Dorothy
Marie Robards.

I get it: Dorothy Jason, Jason Robards.

Well, you know Bram Chastain has to have his clever
little inside pomo jokes.

So wait, I'm confused. Did the Vergiss trial go to the jury?

Yeah, I think this is all back story stuff. I've been seeing
footage from the murder trial, this trial, file footage from
way back when....Yes, please,
and...tequila?...tequila?...Buck, tequila?...never mind. Yeah,
four beers, three shots of Cuervo dressed. Put it on his
tab.

Hey, what? What are you saying about me?

What's the score Buck?

Three nothing, Sweden.

Hey John, you don't really care, do you?

Nah, just messing with him.

So, I'm looking at this trial, you know; so this Vergiss girl killed her best friend after watching *Primal Curse*? That doesn't even make sense.

Yeah, John, what was the rationale here, do you know? I mean, I can't say anything about the movie because I didn't see it, but in the story Dorothy Jason kills her sister. And it's her brother in the movie, right? But the actual murder happens when she's like eight years old. How does Amy Vergiss claim that was her motivation?

I guess the idea was that she was inspired, in some warped fashion, to try and commit the perfect murder. And of course it was anything but. I mean, this girl is one hundred percent pure dumbass. I think it took the cops all of two and a half days to put everything together. So then, from what I read about and saw on TV, she still had this deluded notion that she had somehow perpetrated this genius criminal act, and that by confessing she was only playing out this stupid movie to the end. She's really kind of pathetic.

So, I still don't see, what's the basis of the mom's suit? So her stupid daughter does something she saw on TV; that's Lifetime's fault? Maybe the victim's family should sue this crazy lady for sucking as a parent.

Who knows, Sybil, maybe they will. Apparently, some lawyer and Amy's mom have managed to convince one another that the makers of the movie are responsible by virtue of the fact that they idealized Dorothy Jason to the point that her actions are not merely excusable, but worthy of emulation. It's like she has to kill somebody in order to become this virtuous.

This is ridiculous. Let Mom sue Lifetime, maybe Lifetime can sue the victim's family, *Texas Monthly* can sue Bram Chastain for plagiarism, Bram Chastain can sue his publisher for assigning an editor that couldn't see all this coming. Then the publisher can sue Skip Hollandsworth for the temptation of Brad Chastain. Hell, maybe Marie Robards could sue the whole bunch of them for something or other. Why not?

So then, where are the rightful heirs of Shakespeare and Poe in all of this?

Yeah, it kind of makes me wonder if Bram Chastain isn't sketching out a sequel as we speak. Wait a minute, looks like we might have a verdict. Seems ace courtroom correspondent Francine Garman is about to deliver the news. Can anybody read the captioning?

So yeah, I think so. Let's see..."IN A DECISION NO ONE SURPRISE..." What the?...Hey! I can't see! Buck! Sit down!

Yeah! Whoo hoo!

So, wait a minute, here we go..."A CASE WORTH THE OF SHAGS PEER WHOSE AID TWO BEE ARE NOT TUBE EASE..."   Good grief, who transcribes this stuff? And what does that have to do with anything?

Well Sybil, I'm sure it signifies nothing. She just wanted to throw in a Shakespeare quote to class things up a bit, and that's the one everybody knows.

More important to look smart than put in the effort of actually having a real thought, right John?

Why Nikki, you become more jaded by the moment. I think I'm falling in love. So have we figured out who the winner is in all this yet?

Sweden baby! Three nothing! Yeah!

Precious Moon Circle

Amy LaBonte

Prescott was driving up from Rhode Island. Marci set out the ingredients for roast duck, squash, bread pudding, salad with almonds.

He'll add the wine, she thought. *White hair, blue eyes, a noble face, skin thin and silky.* She smiled. He was also aging.

She talked him into coming. He was hesitant about the drive, his workload. All excuses, she knew.

She could never compete with his ex-wife. Marci's tight drugstore-brown curls, her shapeless pants that reached just above protruding ankle bones would never measure up to Prescott's platinum ex-stunner.

Even if the ex did manage to muster an exotic chronic ailment. Prescott had to cradle the woman's head for nights and months on end. It might have snapped off her neck otherwise. The head.

Marci heard all the stories about her, and about the wonder child conceived late in Prescott's life. She met the child once and traveled to Rhode Island twice. Otherwise, she and Prescott met at Marci's place only, on Friday or Saturday nights, and never both in a row.

Marci hummed Frank Sinatra tunes as she cooked and baked. She headed down the hall to the front room which overlooked the street with the gently waving trees. She scanned the shadows for movement.

There were no rugs in her apartment. Candles emphasized the lonely feel of night.

At eight o'clock the doorbell rang.

"I'm coming," Marci yelled as she raced down the flight of stairs, her voice zany and echoing throughout the three-decker building.

She opened up to him, fell into his arms.

Prescott's strong hands undid her grip from around his neck. But she ignored that with her free-flowing talk and laughter.

Like a giddy dizzy child she led him upstairs. "Sit, eat."

She served him salad with expensive oil drizzled over the arranged leaves and slivers of the best cheese.

Prescott talked about his day, about some clients who wanted to sue him.

Marci was intent on hearing about the negatives in his life. The positives gave her chills.

He paused. "It all smells wonderful."

She laughed. "It should, I've been at it for hours."

He told her a quick story, to fill the time perhaps. "I received a letter today, an old college gal pal sent me a short letter, just to say hello, and there in the envelope is a picture she's had taken, her portrait I suppose..."

Marci continued chewing.

"Well, that photo," he harrumphed. "Here I'm remembering a 20-year old girl and instead come face-to-face with a woman of a certain age wearing lipstick!"

Marci blushed. She had made herself up for this evening, a rare thing, mascara and lip gloss.

"She looked so awfully old," Prescott continued. "The lipstick did her in, though the total effect, hair too long, dowdy clothes, aging face, all put me into shock."

Prescott abruptly stopped speaking.

Quick, change the subject! "Trip. To Italy." Marci leaned forward and gushed, "Tuscany. I found a wonderful inn, we can leave in two weeks. The weather will be perfect."

Prescott cleared his throat. "That won't be possible. I have something to tell you."

She interrupted. "No – I mean! Can we talk about some kind of trip at least? It doesn't have to be so soon."

"I must tell you something," Prescott insisted. "It may come as quite a shock. I don't know how you will react."

Her ribcage turned to stone.

"Oh Prescott," she whispered, love in her eyes. Love, longing, sorrow, dismay, hope. Maybe he had a disease that she could cure, or perhaps see him through. She picked up her wine, steadied her hand.

"I'm getting married. My fiancée is on her way over from China."

Marci choked first, then let out a fake laugh. "Whaaaat?" Her voice might have sounded gleeful in a disastrous parallel universe.

"She's a wonderful woman." Prescott looked out the longitudinal window. "She has a child also, the same age as my little girl, and we're going to start a real family together."

Marci blinked hard. "A woman from China?"

"Her name is Hanna, a translation from the Chinese," Prescott instructed, at first forgetting that he was speaking to the woman whom he was scorning, then catching himself and looking away. "She's in her thirties –

young enough to, well, continue having children, which I welcome so much."

Marci pictured a tall Eurasian beauty, multi-lingual, completely and undeniably exceptional. Everything Marci was not.

Prescott had been taken with things Chinese for a while. He'd even traveled there on business not long ago. Marci heard through the grapevine that Prescott was smitten with the uncommon, not that Marci needed to be reminded. She knew so well his fascinations.

"We've had a good run, you and I." Prescott pushed his chair back and stood. With an earnest face, he headed to her side of the table. "But – it was friendship. I'm moving on to have a real family again."

He bent over. Marci lay her face in the crook of his neck. She breathed in his odor, his blood.

Oh ,why couldn't she cry?

The two of them unlocked from one another as if on cue.

Prescott left the room and returned with his windbreaker already zipped on. "Will you see me out?"

"You don't have to go. What about my bread pudding?"

"I just can't, Marci."

She followed him down the long hall and stairwell. He kissed her on the cheek, said "take care." He skipped down the front stone stairs.

Her knees buckled. She went upstairs and extinguished all the candles, spent the night in darkness.

Over the weekend she kicked her legs, punched the mattress, had fits, then played dead. She avoided her roommates who had real careers, families in distant places, parties with colleagues, papers to grade, boyfriends, ex-husbands, Halloween, Veteran's Day, and all the rest of the observable holidays.

Marci filled her emptiness with a rabid resignation. She drove out to windy cold and dirty beaches, barren places not far from home. She trekked to outposts in her old red Volvo, pondered the usual garbage, now frozen into the iceberg sand. All was the color of bile, even the sky.

Nobody looked at her anymore, not even store clerks. She was as invisible as a star washed away by the city lights.

#

It was still snowing in late April. Marci walked home from her job as a secretary at M.I.T. She watched the flakes dislodge themselves from the palm of the sky.

Then she slammed into something.

She fell backwards. A hand reached for her. Guitar Man! Marci was surprised by his strength first, then by his open features. His eyes were upon her. Brown warm eyes.

"We meet again," he said. "It's been a lonely winter. How about that hot chocolate?"

They had collided in front of the 1439 Jazz Café.

Inside people were safe and warm.

"My, oh my." Marci sipped her whipped chocolate drink. "I guess I'm stuck in a time capsule; the world has gone on without me."

Guitar Man nodded in agreement. "I know how it is. I'm divorced with a son... Only tragedies bring you into the future."

Guitar Man's name was Wilson and he lived close by, as did Marci. They decided to go out on a proper date the next night even though they barely knew one another.

But the snow intensified into a blizzard. Chest-high drifts stopped traffic. Marci and Wilson had to postpone meeting. On the phone Marci asked Wilson if he was seeing anybody.

"No," he said. "Not really."

Marci left it at that.

After she hung up the phone rang again.

"Hello, it's me. Prescott."

She didn't miss a beat. "Are you married yet?"

"No. May I see you?"

"When?" She was thinking of Wilson.

"I'll be there in two hours. Just give me two hours."

"But there's a blizzard," Marci objected. "The roads are closed."

He had already hung up.

#

Prescott sipped tea in Marci's square living room.

"I've met someone," Marci declared.

Prescott put his arm around her shoulders. "I'm both sorry for myself and happy for you."

Marci glared at him.

"Hanna..." Prescott began, picking through his words, "Hanna is not quite -- what you, I, would have expected." His blue eyes scanned Marci's face. "She's an Oriental, Mongolian. Very hard to read."

"Ahhhh." Marci played along. "And that means...?"

"We get along, as do our children. But I may have gotten into another situation... Like the one with my ex -- we were building a sensational relationship and then it came crashing down, with her illnesses, then her wanting to leave me."

Marci stood.

"Surely I can just sleep on your couch tonight?" Prescott asked.

"What about the children?"

"They are with their respective mothers."

"Well, since you've made such an effort to get here..." Marci inquired no further of Hanna.

Prescott carried her to the bedroom.

They kept the lights off and fumbled perfectly. They were used to this routine of gratification.

In the morning Marci woke first. She snuck out to the front room. The streets were cleared and the sky shone a wet blue. The bright snow narrowed the world with caverns and towers.

Prescott came up behind her. "Can't go home now."

Marci turned to him. "You're not leaving? Look, the streets are plowed."

Prescott remained detached and fixed. Water, stone. That's how she saw him: a beautiful fountain, for show and for meditation, built on someone else's land.

"I'm making us breakfast." Prescott marched into the kitchen in the terry cloth robe that wasn't his (it belonged to Marci but was a size extra-large) and whipped eggs. Marci's eyebrows knit and crocheted above her wrinkly eyes.

They ate in silence.

"So, what now with you and the mail order bride?" Oops, this was the first time Marci let on about what she really thought.

The robe was fraying. Prescott's fine hair caught in some loops of fabric. He laughed. "How did you know?"

Marci excused herself.

She closed the bedroom door and telephoned Wilson. He suggested lunch at a place in a rebuilt part of Cambridge. Marci thought the modern streets and architecture there unyielding, fit for emptiness, for the scattering of crowds. But she agreed.

Prescott had cleaned up: the dishes hand-washed and dried, table and floor wiped down.

"Going out?"

"Yes, I am." She offered no explanation.

Prescott went to dress. When he was ready to return to his other life, he asked, "May we continue seeing one another?"

"Maybe."

They kissed good-bye. All the sweetness in their mouths came from Marci's toothpaste tube.

She decided to walk to the meeting place. Passing through her neighborhood, she realized that she had grown old there: well, only her eighty-five year old aunt believed she was not old, but Marci knew better. Marci had seen windowless pubs turn into tapas boutiques and lesbian cafés, permit parking signs posted at every corner, iron fences around triplexes kept rust-free. No dogs went stray, no drunks fell onto the swept sidewalks. Through all the gentrification, the families, whether foul-mouthed or educated, kept some patch of grass green, and hope alive. That's what families did.

Marci didn't miss her own family. Her life went by moment by moment. *I'm not bitter*, she thought. *I'm open to the unknown. I'm going to meet Wilson now at a fancy joint, a restaurant far beyond my psychological means and never before considered an option.*

She stood at the entrance to the expensive restaurant, at the crossroads of wide alien streets. The buildings had no side alleys.

The doormen flicked their eyes at Marci, just as they flicked their cigarettes, first furtively tapping the ashes away from their bodies, then quickly inhaling, one more time: inhale, then flick! The cigarettes landed in the gutter. Marci watched them not conceal their habit -- and they didn't care that she watched. They were young and she was not.

"Coming through, boys!" She clomped past them.

Surprised, they opened the heavy double doors.

The haughty hostess, a stylish girl in the uniform du jour and beaucoup jewelry, ignored Marci.

"Hello," Marci said. "Hello!"

The hostess used her trained muscles to turn on her work face: smile and don't blink. "Yes?"

"I'm meeting someone here... A man – Wilson. Has he arrived?"

"Just one second ." The hostess looked down at a massive book.

Marci heard her name, a bleating sheep sound, then clatter, mumble, mumble. Marci stuck her arm up in the air. *He'll see this!*

Wilson rescued her, escorted her through the loud talking and clanking, the yum yum of being seen.

"It's too loud in here," he yelled into her ear.

Their faces were close. She was ecstatic to see his features so magnified.

She persisted in her uninhibited study of his delicate nose, oily skin, breathing lips, as he steered her through the huge dining area. She liked being steered. She didn't have to look anywhere but at him, into him.

He stopped at a table. "Marci, I want to introduce you to an old friend."

A blank-faced woman was about to dip French bread flesh into a cat's saucer of deep green herbs.

Wilson pulled out Marci's chair. "Nubia, meet Marci. Marci, Nubia."

Nubia smiled, extended her hand. Marci did the same. Nubia's hand felt slim like a garden snake. Nubia pulled back and one of her bulky rings caught on the fabric of Marci's glove. They struggled to disengage.

Nubia's unruffled chignon highlighted her white skin. She wore an expensive sweater. Marci could tell by the perfect fit and softness of it, the unusual color.

Marci did not remove her pre-owned coat or the wool stocking around her head.

"We were waiting for you," Wilson said.

"Have you known Wilson long?" Nubia dipped another piece of bread.

"Not really."

Why is Wilson not talking? "Your name," Marci said in an effort to get through her astonishment, "it's so unusual."

"Oh, I changed it long ago. It's a traveling name. I travel quite a bit. Wilson hasn't mentioned it?"

The waiter arrived and attempted to hand Marci one of those billboard menus but she kept her gloved hands in her lap. He lay the shiny maybe greasy tablet atop Marci's plate.

"Nubia surprised me just after you and I spoke." Wilson was creating a disaster with his cocktail napkin, bunching it up then shredding it. "Nubia and I go way back..."

Nubia smiled. She showed her thin teeth. Those teeth reminded Marci of a possum. "Yes, but I've been abroad. I've been living in Milano, you know, Italia -- but my assignment has ended. Anyway, I've decided to settle back in Cambridge. It's where Wilson and I first met. We were married at one time, you know."

Marci's face went numb. "No, I didn't know."

"Of course back then I wasn't in love with him." Nubia looked over at Wilson. She placed her veinless hand on his arm. "Isn't that right darling? Wilson was always brooding back then. Into himself, digging within. What have you found my precious?"

Wilson stared at the table, at the crumbs and strands of his shredded paper napkin.

Marci's thoughts flew to Prescott. She shouldn't have been so strong with him. He might have spent the day. This Nubia, that Hanna, both probably quite similar: unyielding yet fevered, and flawed.

"I have to go." Marci stood. She pushed her chair back and it fell onto a neighbor's back.

Marci rushed out, wool scarf falling from her head, its loops unwinding and sweeping over the restaurant patrons' nouvelle foods.

The doormen were stomping their black sneakers into the sanded pavement. They were still smoking.

"Leaving so soon?" One of them, cynical and blank, eyebrows raised, spit out a slim cyclone of smoke and steam.

Wilson came running. "Please Marci, don't go. Come back. Nubia is just a ---"

"I have one of those in my life also," Marci interrupted. The doormen snickered.

"Good-bye Wilson." She waved, leaving him there to deal with the condescending men and women, buildings, money talk, the perverse poetry of skill and luck.

#

Marci allowed Prescott to visit her once a week. He drove up from Rhode Island on Friday nights since Hanna spent every weekend with her Chinese group, for international trade purposes. Prescott's ex-wife took both kids. Neither Marci nor Prescott discussed his life beyond these simple facts.

Marci was secretly convinced that Prescott would soon separate from Hanna.

#

"Oh look it's Precious Moon," Marci said.

Marci and Prescott were headed to the trolley, on their way to a party hosted by Marci's friends, that same group of people she'd known for thirty years, most paired off, some looking pretty played out, a few occasionally bringing fresh blood to the group and that fresh blood intermingling and staying on to further engorge the circle. The party was in honor of Marci's reunion with Prescott.

Marci called out, "Precious Moon!"

"Precious who?" Prescott squinted over at a sylph woman wearing layers of faded sweats. He saw a battered lean-to and suffering animal displays.

"Surely you don't know that person?" Prescott took Marci by the arm and turned her away from the radical woman's orbit.

Marci was thrilled that Prescott was touching her and talking to her.

"No, let's go meet her," Marci insisted. She placed Prescott's arm around her shoulders and wound her own arm around his waist. She urged him towards the cat stand.

"Oh come now, Marci. We're not really going over there?"

Marci laughed. "Prescott, don't be afraid!"

They stood entwined before the makeshift stand. Leaflets and sign-up sheets were spread out, a jar had change in it. A gaunt Precious Moon was yelling at to the Saturday evening crowd, "Homeless cats need your help!"

Marci waved her free arm in an exaggerated manner though she was only a few feet away. "Precious Moon! Hello, I know you!"

Wilson and Marci had first met at the cat stand so many months before. He was carrying a guitar slung over his shoulder. He asked her out but she was cooking that last meal for Prescott.

"Marci please! We'll be late." Prescott's forehead creased in discomfort. He tried to free himself but Marci held on tightly.

She wished the moment would last forever.

For appearance's sake, Prescott patted Marci on the back. Tap, tap, each pat sent his palm farther away from her.

"Precious Moon, are you saving cats?" Marci asked.

Precious Moon pulled a cigarette from a semi-crushed pack on the table. She lit the crooked cigarette and blew smoke towards Marci and Prescott. Prescott fanned the air around his face.

Precious Moon pointed at the signs and placards; she stabbed a finger at each of the enlarged photos of distressed cats. "You see these? These cats are the losers in this game humans play and I'm here to be a voice for them. Can you understand, can you help? Money is the answer, money, names, signatures, all of it. Sign the sheets, give twenty dollars."

Prescott's face was patched with pink hives. He disengaged himself from Marci's hold. "It's time to go." He walked away without her.

Marci shrugged her shoulders at Precious Moon. She felt she should say something, or maybe offer money. She searched for her wallet when she heard her name.

A hand caressed her shoulder.

Marci whirled around. She saw Wilson. He was her height. She forgot about that.

They hugged. Wilson's narrow body felt so different from Prescott's. Marci thought she could possibly lift Wilson, he was that slight and light, and swing him around in a joyful reunion dance.

Then, like black magic, Nubia's face appeared, eyes elongated with unbroken eyeliner drawn like Egyptian markings on a gold mask. She wore a striped boat neck top and thick anchor earrings. Her hair was pulled into its French twist with not a stray hair or conspicuous bobby pin to mar its defiant construction. She refused to look at Marci, stared with a trumpet face at Wilson.

Prescott appeared. "My name is Prescott," he said to Nubia and held out his hand. She gave him a once over, then offered her hand. Both hands remained locked until Marci and Wilson disengaged.

"Marci and I were on our way to a party," Prescott added, still ogling Nubia. He was not interested in who, what or where. All he cared about was why not.

Everyone waited.

"Let's all go together." Marci surprised herself.

Prescott and Nubia led the way. Nubia in her sailor outfit pranced to Prescott's clipped flaxen utterings.

Wilson and Marci didn't move. They watched their significant others become engrossed in new adventure, watched the newly-formed couple get swallowed up by the crowd. The sun had just left the sky. Twilight was rising from the ashen streets.

Side by side Wilson and Marci lingered, their gazes, as if by habit, still focused on the disappearance of their loved ones.

Wilson's fingers found Marci's hand. What had they been thinking? They looked at one another. Wilson began singing: *Love and happiness...Love and happiness...You be good to me...I'll be good to you...We'll be together...We'll see each other...* Wilson swung Marci's arm back and forth, his voice pitch perfect and getting stronger.

The sidewalk became the couple's special cloud. Precious Moon grabbed a hidden placard, moved around the table and stood with the couple. The placard glowed violet in the coming night. Precious Moon raised and lowered the placard as she hummed along. The passers-by formed a constantly shifting circle around the three of them.

Precious Moon's placard said, *We Won!* in anticipation of the cessation of all suffering.

The three discarded people laughed and hugged.

2013

Miriam Sachs

"I got it working. Maybe come 2013 we'll get a new TV that doesn't take me a half an hour to set up." Tamara ate her dinner at the coffee table, tuning in to the New York Broadcast. The ball would drop in seven minutes. The New Year would leak in through the windows and all of a sudden, nothing would change. Except, a number would grow by one. Tamara and Daniel would have to get used to writing the date with a thirteen at the end instead of a twelve.

Daniel sat beside Tamara on the ruined gray sofa. He laid his paper plate next to hers and reached for the silverware.

"I forgot a fork," he said. Daniel wiped his hands on fleece sweatpants. He smothered his face with Costco chicken until the chicken's skin was the only thing left on the plate. Finally stopping to breathe, Daniel wiped his greasy hands on fleece sweatpants. "Don't need a fork," he said, with food in his mouth.

"New Years Resolutions?" said his wife.

"None for me," he said.

"No, yours is, 'I will not forget my fork again.'" Tamara giggled for less than a second. Then she stopped and stared in abrupt interest at a tall, blonde, heavily made-up announcer on the TV.

"2013 won't be any different," Daniel said. "It just reminds everybody that you don't stay young and frozen like a picture. The moments run out, and you're always back to your work. It reminds you that seconds are wasting, and that you better do something important because otherwise history will pass right by Mr. Daniel D. Weiss, accountant, without dawdling for dessert."

"You're right," Tamara said. "Dates mean accomplishments measured in three-sentence blurbs. The date is just to look back on. We could stay in 2012 and it wouldn't make a difference to us. Just to the people in the future who live for three hundred years and mark events in their e-textbooks by the month and year. Although I suspect months will be eliminated when you're that old, just like pennies will be too."

"Four minutes until 2013. Go America, we've survived for over two-thousand years," Daniel said. "Mr. Greyfield three doors down told me he doesn't believe it."

Tamara kept her eyes on the shiny globe. "What?" she said.

"He's a kook. Thinks history's just a hullabaloo of spies working for the government. I was just saying a friendly Happy New Year and he told me he doesn't believe it. Government spies just made up that date. Then he said Earth was around before we made up when the year starts and when it ends. He told me nobody knows when the Earth began and even if we did, it probably began over a long period of time, a couple hundred years, not a second at midnight. The government apparently uses the date to control us? I don't know. Pretty funny though." Daniel snorted, his version of a laugh. He sounded like a fan at a football game when the other team scores a touchdown.

"Makes sense," Tamara related. "Except for the government spies. But like I said, might as well be 2012. It's just a number. And besides, thirteen is unlucky."

"Now you've jinxed us both."

Tamara smiled, "And the whole world."

Daniel left the living room for more food. The toaster dinged.

"You'll miss the ball drop," she called.

"Yeah, yeah," said a muffled voice from the kitchen.

Daniel was back at a minute to the New Year. "We're out of bread." He made a mess of buttering his toast so that the crumbs gave the sofa a shower and ensured that the vacuum would make an appearance in the morning. Spreading butter was hard to do without a knife.

"I'll go to Ralph's in the morning. We need more eggs too," said Tamara.

There was no more speech after that. Husband and wife glued their eyes to the television behind two paper plates side by side on the wooden coffee table. For 58 seconds, all was as expected.

Then, at one second until 2013, the TV stopped. About ten seconds ticked by, but the image stayed with the ball just above the ground. There was no confetti, no excited final announcement, no half-hearted cheering from the couple on the sofa.

"It froze up!" Tamara cried. "We need a new TV."

"Don't sweat it. I'm tired anyway. We'll deal with it tomorrow." Daniel took the plates back to the kitchen. "This clock's broken here too," he said.

"Tomorrow!" Tamara groaned. She turned off the TV with the remote beside her, and the colorful screen obeyed, turning in a flash to black. They waddled into bed, squinting in the darkness, fighting drooping eyelashes.

#

Around eight in the morning, just before breakfast, Tamara decided to drive to Ralph's. She would pop in and out, just in time to make omelets when Daniel awoke. Her eyes were still tired, and she was only half awake, but the thought of warm breakfast and coffee urged her on. She threw on jeans and a simple green shirt, ready to greet the sun.

In a sleepy daze, she opened the door and walked outside. The sky was dark as night. She blinked and stammered back. Where was the sun?

Tamara's mouth opened and closed. A shy whimper dribbled from her lips, and fingers rushed urgently to her hair, flattening her curls into long brown streaks against her cheek. She turned back to get her husband, but remembered Daniel was still asleep.

Again she looked up to the sky. A gaping darkness stared down at her. It drained the color from her cheeks, and the rest of her line of vision too. Stars sat in their miniature thrones, dangling above her like chandelier shards. Everything was in order, except that it was night. In some of the houses across the street, the lights were on.

Everything was quiet. Not a calm, peaceful stillness like the nurturing veil of nature, but an immortal, pervading silence that stung. It was a deep, dark slap in the face, a dead blackout, an absence of motion, of life.

On the sidewalk across the street, Jonathan Greyfield walked his dog. Only he wasn't walking. He was in the middle of walking. Even the dog crouched, frozen, eternally sniffing under a white fence with the end of his tail pointed into the air. Tamara's eyes turned to colossal boulders above her nose. Growing, drowning out the rest of her face in terror.

Tamara was right. There would be no New Year after all.

The Time is Snow

Jim Meirose

Snow, snow. The river knows the taste of snow. Gut in the snow. See now. Practical matters; in the hole, down the wars, in the time of war. Just think of it. First time's always the best, for anything. The truck mowed down the asphalt on the Interstate. In the windshield. There's no need to stop. I mean there's no need to stop. Push the brake. The green light on the dash tells you you keep on drivin'. With freepass. In the muck; the mud is dry as a herd in the field. The herd slowly moved across the field lowing low. He raised the shotgun. It's hard it's damned hard. Nervy aren't you. Just drip the feeling lions share. Heartly comes in the flying fish. Praying the Fishlist. How the mods and rockers rock and how the field in the park plays down. In the frying pan in to the place I must type it I must— you're mother's a psycho. I sit eating the stuff down and you really gagged up the salad honey. It's almost eight o'clock. The clock is striking eight but it's fast. It's not eight. It's almost eight. The white lines flow by. One two three four five six seven eight. Picky picky picky picky. Do the plates. Do the plates, Steck. Shoes off, Steck. Wild he goes. The pour is drying off the game. The pour is drying.

Time to do the pour. Hoover dam. Inside Hoover dam. Dry the game of the neck of the Berliner.

I sit eating the stuff down. You really gagged up the salad honey. Stun me. Yeah yeah. Use the stun gun. Pow! I sit eating the stuff down. What'd that salad go down the wrong pipe honey?

Fifty Fifty

Timothy Hurley

Nelson saw the combatant's black boot just before it disappeared into the doorway across the street. He raised his rifle and fired. A chunk of stucco and rock exploded near where the boot had been.

"Son-of-a-bitch. Stick your head out next, and I'll blow it off." The edge of a white turban emerged from the doorway about six feet above the ground. As Nelson raised his rifle, it disappeared.

"Bet your ass, pull back, raghead." Nelson coughed to eliminate the tremor in his voice. He let loose a string of epithets he would never have thought to speak in his grandmother's living room in Brooklyn. He shouted an assertion about his adversary's lack of pedigree. He yelled about his opponent's girlfriend and mother, naming them after body parts he never discussed with his priest at St. Charles' Church. And he denigrated his enemy's body parts, screaming how he would cut one of them off after blowing his brains out.

While Nelson yelled, he trembled, and he felt the need to urinate. He leaned his shoulder hard into the wall of the doorway to steady his aim and his nerve. He had the Afghani pinned down in the doorway recess across the street, but at the same time, Nelson was trapped in his entryway. The alley that represented escape for either of them was at least thirty feet of open running from the relative safety of their recessed hiding places. Either of them was certain to take a bullet in the attempt.

Nelson slid down the wall and sat on his butt, holding his rifle between his knees. He leaned far enough to see the other doorway, but saw no movement, and he pressed his back against the cool stucco. The sun was high, and the day would get hotter. He pulled out his canteen, took a swallow, and hoped his adversary didn't have one.

Nelson supposed his squad was at least a mile away by now. Even if they had heard his shot, they wouldn't make anything of it. They had been working their way east in the city when Nelson went down the wrong alley into this deserted neighborhood. He guessed a similar mistake had led the solitary enemy combatant to the same location. Nelson's phone was crushed, and he could not tell anyone he was stuck with someone who wanted him dead. He determined the heavy door, barred firmly from the inside, was not an option. A grenade tossed into the other doorway would end the standoff, but he had none.

Based on the fervor of the screaming he heard from the other doorway, Nelson guessed the Afghani was yelling about Nelson's mother and girlfriend—and cutting off his dick. He snickered and then choked on the laugh. If the two of them encountered each other in a bar in Red Hook, Nelson would challenge him to a chug-a-lug or game of pool. Maybe they would insult each other's girlfriends and end up in a fistfight. And then they would go home at three o'clock in the morning. Here, Nelson knew, a bloody nose would not be a sufficient wound to allow either of them a face-saving exit. For reasons he had never questioned, before one could go home, the other must die.

Nelson hollered into the street, "Hey fuck-face, you know I'm going to blow your head off, right?" He wasn't confident of the truth of that, but shouting bolstered his courage. Except for the word *fuck*, the machine-gun-like torrent of words from across the street was babble to Nelson.

He placed a tremulous thumb on the sight of his rifle, and lowered his voice to a whisper. "Of course, you might blow mine off first…" Then, raising his voice again to a shout, "I'll thank you not to talk about my mama that way, asshole. My mama's a nice lady. So's my grandma. We live in Brooklyn, you know. Near the F-train. That's 'F' for 'fuck you, raghead.' You come to my neighborhood, and I'll blow your fucking brains out." Nelson sniggered, then fell silent. His face went dark, and the memory of the day swamped his mind—the Tuesday, at age eleven, when he stayed home from school, stood hypnotized on a pier, and watched black smoke across the East River surge into blue sky.

Nelson picked up a rock and flung it into the dirt street. "My cousin was in the building, you know…." His next words never made it out of his mouth, obstructed by the same restrained anguish that prevented his tears.

Nelson's thoughts shot to the memorial service at St. Mark's Church in Jersey City. When his aunt fainted, he and his father helped her into the cold air and sat with her on the concrete steps. He told her he would get the bastards who killed her

Sammy, but she patted his hand and said there was enough dying.

***

Nelson woke, and his head jerked up hard and slammed the back of his helmet against the wall. His heart hammered in his chest, his ears rang, and he sucked in and stopped breathing

How long had he dozed? Had his cover been compromised? Where was the Afghani?

He thrust his head round the corner and looked left and right and into the alley. He saw nothing. There was only the hot stink from the street. The sun had moved, but not much. His ears struggled to hear a boot scrape the ground from the other doorway—any sound would reassure him. But he heard nothing.

Moving in quick jerks, he swung out of the doorway, raised his rifle to his shoulder, and fired at the doorway. An explosion of rock and plaster broke the silence.

"Come on out, shit-head." Nelson recognized the desperation in his own voice.

A brown face appeared behind a rifle across the street. Nelson heard a crack and the ground exploded next to his left boot. He felt a pain in his ankle, as if a scalpel were being dragged across it. But he didn't look. He aimed and fired just as the face was disappearing behind the stucco.

"Still there, you bastard? Fell asleep too?" Nelson slid down the wall, laid his rifle on the stone floor, and looked at the thick red ooze that mixed with the dust on his boot. His heart continued to pound, and he was surprised that the pain stopped. He unlaced his boot, changed his mind, and tied it up again. The canteen was nearly empty, but he took a swallow, and splashed water on his face and neck.

"Getting thirsty, raghead? Come on over. I'll kick your ass." His words lacked the vehemence of his earlier bellowing. The heat and strain sapped his hostility, the way, back home, the July sun turned mud puddles to cracked dirt. Maybe he should have listened to his mother, he thought. Maybe his aunt was right. He relaxed his back against the wall and touched the drying blood on his boot.

The yelling from the other doorway was slower, less intense. Perhaps he's exhausted too, Nelson thought. He wanted it to be over, wished he were someplace else—home at his grandmother's dinner table.

"What's that, Omar? You wanna know about Brooklyn? Great place, Brooklyn. Come see. I'll shoot your friggin' head off.... Sometimes I walk to Flatbush and get kabobs. You like kabobs, Omar? You getting hungry? I'm hungry."

"Behnam."

"Whatzat, Omar?"

"Behnam. Nah Omar."

"Behnam? That's your name? Hey, the guy in the bodega near our apartment is Behnam. Small world, Behnam. Nelson. My name's Nelson. Too bad we have to come here and blow your country back to the Stone Age." Nelson chuckled. "But from what I can tell, you weren't so far from it." He picked up a pebble, peered round the corner, and tossed it into the street. Presently, a brown nose poked past the other doorway and a similar pebble flew into the street, coming to rest not far from Nelson's.

Nelson leaned back against the wall. "So, Behnam, you got a girl here? I got a girl. We were going to get married, but she wanted to wait. She figured I had a fifty-fifty chance of getting back to Red Hook in a bag. Bad odds, she said. Didn't want to be a widow." Nelson laughed and wrung his fingers. "My Mom thought I was stupid signing up, but my Dad said someone had to avenge cousin Sammy. Sometimes I wish it didn't have to be me, know what I mean?"

Behnam picked it up, and Nelson went silent. The words made no sense to him, but the cadence and rhythm made him feel as if he were being told a story. He recognized the word 'maamaan-bozorg'.

"Maamaan-bozorg? Your grandmother?"

"Maamaan-bozorg."

"Yeah, well, Behnam, my maamaan-bozorg makes the best damn cherry pie in New York. You ever had cherry pie? She uses fresh cherries, you know? Tastes like… paradise… know what I mean?"

"Pardis, baleh."

"Right, paradise…. How are we going to get out of here, Behnam? You going to shoot me if I get up and walk away?"

More words Nelson did not understand.

"I mean, isn't this crazy?" Nelson squirmed and shifted from one side of his butt to the other. "Do I really gotta kill you to get outta here?" He slapped his rifle barrel. "Do I have to shoot a guy I don't even know?" He rubbed his knees and legs. "I mean, who gives a shit…?" Nelson's mouth was dry, and he licked his lips. "I mean, if I'm going home in a bag, then that's it, right? If that's what's gonna happen, shouldn't we get on with it?"

The street fell quiet, and the sun descended into the west. Nelson got up and paced, and his mind leaped from the dirt road in front of him to his grandmother's living room, to the church steps at Sammy's memorial, to rows of black zippered bags in a hangar.

He peered round the corner, then squatted and retrieved his rifle; he fingered the safety and sights. "Hey, Behnam, it's going to get dark soon. It doesn't look like my guys or your guys are coming back. You know we each have a fifty-fifty chance of leaving here alive, right?"

Silence.

"Behnam?"

"Naylson?"

Nelson stamped and clenched his jaw. He kicked the wooden door, and slapped the stucco. "Goddamit all to hell. I've had enough of this shit. It's insane. I'm outta here. Walkin' or bagged. What's it gonna be, Behnam? Let's get this over."

Without contemplation, without reasoning, Nelson took his rifle by the barrel in his left hand and stepped away from the recess into the street. Right arm stretched out, palm forward, he limped to the middle of the road and stopped. His legs were apart, and the ripped leather of his left boot was bathed in dried blood. Under his helmet, his unshaven face was grave, expectant. The green and brown and tan of his camouflage uniform were stained with sweat.

Behnam's face appeared—brown and youthful, serious and fearful. He stepped away from his shelter, his rifle butt against his right shoulder, his left hand cradling the barrel.

Nelson squatted, laid his rifle on the street, and resumed his upright position; his arms were stretched wide, palms facing the tip of Behnam's rifle barrel. Nelson watched him rest his cheek on the rifle butt, and saw his left eye squint and his right eye look at him over the gun-sight.

Nelson thought, He can't be more than seventeen. I'm going to be killed by a seventeen year old, halfway around the world from my own neighborhood, and no one is going to know who did it. Nelson pitied the person who would have to avenge his death.

He realized he wasn't breathing, and he filled his lungs. He slapped himself on the chest. "Come on, motherfucker. Every day, it's fifty-fifty—you or me. I've had enough of this shit. Get it over with. It's…. Do it." He slapped his chest again.

In the next moment, Behnam, shaking, looked down, moved the rifle from his shoulder, squatted, and laid the gun on the ground. Then, still trembling, he took two steps toward Nelson. Nelson dropped his arms and stepped forward. They stood within feet of each other. Nelson stared hard into Behnam's brown eyes, and Behnam returned the gaze.

"Assalaamu alaikum," Behnam said, his voice quavering.

"And with you."

The setting sun turned the stucco walls orange and red. Nelson and Behnam backed up, squatted, and retrieved their rifles. They stood and breathed, inhaling air from the fetid street. And each turned away and walked in opposite directions down the alleyway.
Nelson swung round, "Tell your maamaan-bozorg, 'hi'." Behnam turned, showed his white teeth, and resumed walking.

The Saboteur

David Rowland

It's strange, the little things you notice when your mind
should really be concentrating on more important
matters, such as life and liberty. Here I am being bundled
into the back of a car to be taken away forever and all I
can think about as I say goodbye to the world, is the way
the walls of my little granite house sparkle in the
morning sun.

Some people might not notice such insignificant details
others might highlight the peeling paintwork and bare
wood windowsills, the fading yellow fascia. It seems I
have been maintaining my sanity at the expense of my
property, but the little garden out the back is a picture,
Agapanthus and rambling roses. As the black sedan, with
me in the back, pulls out of the street and drives through
the almost empty seaside town I can only wonder what
will happen to my house and my secret garden now I am
gone away.

Looking back I suppose it was a bit daft to think I could
get away with it forever but we humans are nothing if not
optimistic to the point of blind in the face of the obvious.
Now I find myself replaying the past few hours over and
over in my head as I note the morning sunlight filtering
through my grubby net curtains and hear the almost
forgotten authoritarian rap of a firm knockety-knock-

knock-knock on my old wooden front door. No one does that anymore. Knocks on doors I mean, why would you. Not nowadays.

But I have no doorbell, just an old brass knocker, so I am already unusual. But that's not a crime...yet. I decide to answer the summons since supposedly, I'm not hiding anything. On the doorstep I find a grey suited lady with a badge, a bloke in a blue suit and a young policeman all waiting on the pavement before asking can they come in, have a 'brief word' and 'a quick look round'? I am feeling less than co-operative.

'Bit busy actually...' I explain and go to close the door. The policeman pulls out his tele-cosh and looks at Blue Suit, who shakes his head and then asks me politely in an oily sort of way, foot already well wedged in the doorway, 'Mr Peter Bowman?' I nod.

What else can I do? I'm too old to run for it and where would I run to? As yet there is no sensation of alarm. No bells ring, maybe the batteries have gone flat. Blue Suit has what some call a 'ruddy' complexion and, of all things, a huge handlebar moustache. I keep expecting him to shout 'Tally-ho chaps' or 'Roger blue leader, angels one five' but if I said so he probably wouldn't know what I was on about. He's a big bloke so I decide it's probably best not to antagonise him. Then, without further preamble, he just pushes his way in and starts looking round. As if the place is some kind of museum. He noses his way into the front room. 'Is this your lounge?' he asks.

'What's it to you?' I reply, forgetting for a moment that I am trying not to antagonise him. By now however, faint bells are ringing, I think I know what's coming. Blue Suit looks around room with an expression of distaste as if my house smells a bit ripe or something. He looks puzzled. His moustache is twitching like some kind of social weirdo sensitive antennae. He fixes me with his cold blue eyes and then he asks,

'Whereabouts *is* your telewall?'

'I don't have one,' I inform him.

So much for not antagonising him but then I realise I don't care anymore. I had thought that with me being so old they might not bother but now I realise eighty-five isn't really that 'old' and here I am well up shit creek in a barbed wire canoe without a paddle. Next the three of them start going through my house, carefully noting down my various misdemeanours. And I just stand there and let them. Well what else am I going to do, shoot the bastards? I know there's some that do but I'm in enough trouble as it is.

They look in the cupboards, under the bed and even down the toilet and all without so much as a by your leave. They look at my paintings and inspect my 'comfy' slippers, they handle things and 'tut-tut', as if my possessions are, of themselves, a criminal offence. They note that the house has not been decorated 'in several years'. They go out back to see my garden. They ask why is there no neat lawn? My reply mystifies them.

'Never again will I make the neat lawn mistake.'

My garden is the longest in the street. Back in 'the old days' when the air round here reeked of sulphur and fish, the foundry workers used to gamble during 'crib' and if they ran out of money, they would gamble their little bits of land, their gardens. Consequently, the back garden of number twenty seven actually belongs to number thirty one while my next door neighbour's back garden strip is only half as long as mine and so on. It used to be a land agency nightmare but no-one can be arsed any more. What would be the point? It will all be under water soon enough.

When the foundry closed, the gambling ceased, at which point whoever it was that owned number 42, my house, must have been on the crest of a wave. They were either a shrewd gambler or just plain lucky. Maybe it was a lucky house back then but times change. As I am about to learn once the dynamic trio have finished ferreting about and the grey haired lady in grey finally decides to tell me that they have had 'a report'.

'A report,' say I, she makes a tick on her clipboard. A small neat tick I suspect. Outside on the street it's just another day in sunny Cornwall. I am aware of the eyes watching. When I first moved in there were all sorts living down my street; arty types always on about the quality of the light, corduroy haired 'new agers' busy knitting their own yoghurt, gallery owners, various purveyors of tourist tat and pseudo culture, social refugees of all shapes and politics and, here and there, the odd Cornish person, all seeking to defend or define the real Cornwall and all gone and half-forgotten now. Now it seems there are only suspicious scared people, grey ladies, blokes in blue suits, a policeman and 'reports'. Cornwall seems to have has lost its attraction. It is no longer particularly remote and it is certainly too dangerous for the average tourist what with the flash floods, rising sea levels, cliff falls and power failures. Not to mention the sunshine.

'Well two reports, actually,' simpers the clip-board carrying grey lady.

'Indeed. I thought you were yet another delegation from the telewall licence people. They came round twice when I didn't renew the licence for my non-existent telewall receiver. They just couldn't believe it. Nearly tore the bloody house apart they did.'

She gives a nervous grin, more of a twitch really. She is a pinched and skinny thin stick lady, she reminds me of Aunt Vera in the old 'Giles' cartoons. She really ought to have glasses, she even has grey eyes. Maybe she wears contacts, Security Bureau issue. She keeps talking. I think her voice is supposed to be calming but all it is really is irritating.

'Yeees. We have had a report that you may be neglecting yourself Mr Bowman'.

I shrug. 'Neglecting myself....in what sort of way?'

She seems lost for words.

'Well, er... not eating the right sort of food, never going out, always wearing shabby old clothes, shouting at your neighbours and the children in the street, that sort of thing.'

This woman is serious, caution is advised. I must admit that I sometimes shout back at the children who call me names like 'weirdo' or 'poor boy' and throw things. I know I shouldn't but I don't see why they can shout at me and not me at them? But all I say is,

'If I 'never go out' how does anyone out there know what state my clothes are in or what I may, or may not be, eating in the privacy of my own home?'

 A fair point milord and 'a palpable hit sir' methinks but it seems the grey lady and her merry band, have not finished yet. Nor has my new 'friend' in a blue suit. He speaks.

'No need to get angry with us Mr Bowman, just doing our job'.

The grey lady smiles thinly and nods as if in acknowledgement of Blue Suit's wise words. Then she takes her opportunity to include her knight in a blue suit in all the Social Bureau fun. Always up for a bit of the old 'inclusivity' are social workers. Least they always used to be, but times change. I'm sure social workers and social security used to be separate entities but like I say, times change, we can only change with them.

'Ahem' she coughs, delicately holding a grey gloved tiny hand to her tiny grey mouth. 'The other matter is really the concern of this gentleman' she fails to explain, waving a hand in Blue Suit's direction. 'You see,' she continues, 'when we put your name into the national computer system a 'Police Interest' flag came up. It seems the police have been trying to trace you but they have been unable to locate you anywhere in the London area and they were just about to widen their 'net', so to speak...' she smiles at her little pun '....when we contacted them and so this gentleman has come with me to see you. The presence of the other officer is 'routine procedure' you understand?'

I give her my best look. 'Actually no... I don't. There was a time you lot were not allowed to exchange information like that?' I add darkly. Then Blue Suit speaks again.

'So you've been living here like this since your 'retirement', have you Mr Bowman? No wonder we couldn't find you on our local searches. You know you should have registered your move with our central records department don't you?'

'You make it sound as if I've been deliberately evading you?' I counter, whilst noting his reference to my 'retirement'. I was dismissed.' Not a team player' they said.

The four of us are now standing in a circle in the middle of my 'lounge'. I have the feeling that something not good is about to happen. Blue Suit addresses me directly.

'Mr Bowman, it seems you have answered no national or local government on-line enquiries with regard to confirming your official lifestyle for at least ten years. You appear to have no televisual receiver licence. Indeed you have no televisual receiver, no transport, no passport, no record of your retinal signature, no new furnishings whatsoever and it seems you have not decorated in several years. Quite frankly Mr Bowman we can only wonder how you manage to meet your monthly quota's...'

I try to look him in the eye but I can only shrug. 'I spend a lot on my painting and my garden' I say. 'Everything costs so much these days and what with the climate and that...' I trail off. Not many people garden these days. It's considered a somewhat eccentric thing to do. But suddenly Blue Suit changes tack and after a quick word with his puppy dog he turns to me and clears his throat. I feel a sense of foreboding. Then, in his best very best police person voice, like they used to do on the TV, he announces...

'Peter John Bowman I am arresting you in connection with continuing enquiries into the death of one Jayne Dunmore in January 1986. You are not obliged to...' and so on and oh, the relief! So, this is what it's about, that old chestnut again. I can only thank the good lord for his, or her, small mercies. But now they want to search the place. In case I've got Jayne's body stashed away somewhere I suppose. Or a cage filled with her bones.

That was the problem thirty years ago. No body. Well they can search all they like, she is not here. Then I remember something and suddenly I am tense. I am scared.

At eighty-five there's not a lot left that can scare you. What am I looking at here? A five year sentence commuted to three and out in two, might even be home by Christmas next year with luck. Then Blue Suit tells me they have formally re-opened their enquiries into Jayne's disappearance because now a body *has* been found *and* identified. This upsets me. I can't believe it, after all these years. I ask where they found her.

'Where you dumped her of course' my new blue un-friend replies with a nasty grin.

I realise we are about to go all over it again just the same as before only now they have a body. Well, a skeleton I suppose. Truth to tell they have no more evidence than they had before, which was nothing then and is nothing now except now they have definitely got a murder, or so they say. When I ask how she died they smile knowingly like they do when they know you're as guilty as sin but they just can't prove it. Then they tell me they already have enough to have me 'put away' unless I tell them what they want to know. Looking round the house it is 'obvious' my lifestyle is unconventional enough to be classified as 'deviant'. I admit I am a little eccentric but I am essentially harmless.

'That's not how it will sound when we're through with you', Blue Suit assures me.

I imagine setting fire to his handlebars and watching him crash in flames, unable to get his cockpit canopy to slide back as he spirals earthwards.

'I have the right to see a solicitor before being interrogated, surely?'

I am hoping they will take me away soon, far away from the house. Then an idea occurs to me, something that might divert them. I consider it for a while. Then I confess.

'I killed her' I say. 'I found out she was having an affair with some bloke from the office so I smothered her in her sleep and then told everyone she'd just walked out'.

And now I have confessed to a murder that only I know I never done? Why would any sane person do something daft like that? There is of course an obvious answer to that. Everybody is looking so pleased but still no move toward the car. Police-boy is all bustle and papery activity making notes on paper that has now been recycled so many times that I and everybody else here has probably wipe their arses with it twice already.

All the while I am conscious of their plan to search the house. If they do then sooner or later they will want to see a receipts record. It's just routine procedure. But I haven't got one to show them and failure to produce your receipts record is a really serious crime. At present only I know that I am not spending anything remotely like my official quota.

Within the terminology of the 'Compulsory National Personal Consumption Act' my legal position is quite clear. Every registered English citizen must reach, if not actually exceed, his or her imposed spending targets in order to keep the economy afloat. Failure to meet government set levels of consumption for a month or so is acceptable, though technically punishable by either a warning or a fine, but to fail to meet your 'target expenditure' for a full quarter is a much more serious offence, a life sentence job.

My spending has not managed to come anywhere near my targets for the past two years. Since the regulations were legalised in fact. Next to this is my failure to register my residency as an English citizen, another very serious offence, and then there is practising art without a licence, the list just grows and grows. That's why I try to keep a low profile. I just do not want the things that I am supposed to want. The things no sane person can live without. I never did. That's why Jane left me all those years ago.

All I wanted was to paint pictures of Cornish lanes where trees wrap themselves around the road to form dark tunnels, a splash of sunlight on the road ahead, power cables, and telegraph poles against a brooding sky, nothing with any great commercial potential. No ambition Jayne said. So she left. I had no idea what happened to her, had never heard a thing until today but I can imagine. She went to see that Danny from the office. Ten to one *he* killed her. He was well capable of murder. That was part of the allure I suppose. Still, all things being equal, I would rather take the rap for a crime of passion than be labelled an 'Economic Saboteur' which is an offence where 'life' means life.

If they arrest me for murder the trial will be over in hours and then they will forget all about me. No-one will ask me anything anymore. I have confessed. Case closed. File it away then promptly lose it. I will be given a therapist. She will smile. But then she will be paid to smile. All of this goes through my mind as we stand facing each other in my front room. I am anxious to be away from the house. I want to be locked up safe and silent in my cell and be back home by next Christmas. Maybe do some more painting.

Then Blue Suit says,

'Just routine Mr Bowman, but would you mind showing me your latest receipts record'

So now, as they drive me away I find myself wishing they would open the car window to let in some air because that is what I will miss most about the lost and gone forever outside world, the sound of the wind in the trees and the cool feel of the moving air.

Seeing Steve

Anthony Rowe

It's my turn to see Steve. I tentatively inch forward until I am standing above him. He's lying flat, his hands are resting upon his chest, and his eyes are closed. I've seen him in this position before, minus the make-up and the bloated appearance, usually after one of the many long, amusing nights we shared together a long time ago.

My eyes slowly scan his body and come to rest upon his perfectly still face. I stare - looking, hoping, willing against reason that his eyelids will lift and expose a mischievous glint, triggering the familiar, electric smile that will reassure me this whole death scene is just some sort of complicated joke. Of course, his eyes don't open. I continue to stare, and my mind wanders as the funeral home's murmurs fade into the background.

Steve is dribbling the basketball just to the left of the top of the key. He bounces on his feet, intently watching the movements of teammates and defenders. His hair is wet from sweat, and it hangs down in strands of straight black across his forehead. Shoes squeak as players cut and push, flash and react. Steve eyes his defender, who is crouched and looking back up at him. To the uninformed, his defender looks ready for whatever Steve may bring. Steve

assesses his options, takes one last look for the open man,
sees no one, and decides to make his move.

Eyes narrow. Face tightens. Steve leans forward, holding
the ball in front of him. Suddenly he moves to his right,
toward the lane, leaning into his defender with his left
shoulder while dribbling with his right hand. The defender
is on his heels, attempting to react to Steve's movements.

Steve, recognizing that his defender is reeling, jumps to a
sudden stop just inside of the free throw line. The defender
continues toward the basket as Steve rises up, eyes locked
on the target, hair flying, left hand gently pulling away
from the basketball as the right hand rises. Defenders
much taller than Steve come to help their beaten
teammate, but they are too late. Steve's arm fully extends
and his fingertips stretch as he releases the ball. As the ball
rolls off of the fingertips, Steve's wrist snaps forward in a
picture-perfect follow through. Steve gently lands on the
balls of his feet as the ball nestles in to the net.

I snap out of my daydream and realize that there are
others waiting to see Steve. I take one last hopeful look,
but he is still still. The magic has been drained out of
him. I walk away and move to the line that leads toward
his wife and two children.

The line edges forward. My turn will be here soon. I
have not seen Steve's wife since his 30th birthday party
fourteen years ago. I wonder if she will remember me.
Steve's two children stand by their mother, looking dazed
and exhausted, going through the scripted motions and
unscripted emotions. The last time I saw Steve's

daughter, she was two. This is the first time I've seen his son.

Like many friendships, mine with Steve faded slowly over a period of years. One life decision after another guided us toward today and farther away from the friendship we had shared. Marriage. Children. Jobs. He moved. I stayed.

As I wait in line, I think back to the last time that I saw Steve. It was seven years ago, at my father's funeral. There were a few hundred people at the service that day, and about half of them showed up at my brother's house for the reception afterwards. I spoke to so many people that day, and I can't remember much of what I said or what I heard, but I will always remember a quiet moment Steve and I shared at the end of the driveway at the end of the day.

Steve and I are talking about my dad. Steve likes to call my dad by his nickname "Red" (but never to his face). I tell Steve that I feel robbed because my father has been taken away too early at the age of 68. Steve listens patiently and then looks me in the eye and says, "Anth, what you have to remember is that those were 'Red Years'." Steve pauses and a warm smile comes across his face. He then points out to me that my father had packed in more in his 68 years than most could hope to accomplish in much longer lifetimes. I smile. Throughout the day I had laughed at many stories of my dad's exploits, but this is the first smile.

We talk quietly for a few more minutes, and then it's time for Steve to go. We shake hands, and he climbs into his car. I stand at the end of my brother's driveway watching Steve drive away.

I look up from the carpet and realize that it's almost my turn to see Steve's wife. The couple she is talking to walks away, and she turns to me. She smiles warmly and opens her arms.

We speak awkwardly in hushed tones for a few minutes, and then it's someone else's turn to share their condolences. I move away. I survey the funeral home, and I see, off at the far end of the room, hand-made posters on easels. I am drawn to the pictures on those posters. I am drawn to the life they document.

The pictures on the posters range from early childhood through last week. In each picture, whether Steve is younger or older, his eyes tell the story. Those eyes put the punctuation mark on any word or action of Steve's. Energy sparked from those eyes. Now, across the room, those eyes are shut tight and I wonder where the light has gone.

I look closely at a picture of Steve from about 20 years ago, and I am taken back.

I'm lying on the couch at my dad's townhouse. It's mid-afternoon on a weekday. The radio is on, but I'm not really listening. I'm supposed to be looking for a job, but I can't, or I won't. Anyway, I don't. Steve walks in without knocking. He is also supposed to be looking for a job. He walks up, sits down, smiles, and asks me what we're going to do. Soon I am up off of the couch and we go. We play hoops, we go to the bowling alley to play Frogger, we go to a movie. I know I will have to face my dad at the end of yet another wasted day; but I'm with Steve and we are laughing, and that pervasive, nameless feeling that lives inside of me is gone for now.

I stand in the middle of the crowded funeral home. I blink back tears as I realize how much I value those wasted days. Steve had lifted me up, time after time after time, at a point in my life when I could have easily stayed down.

#

It's late night/early morning. I'm lying in bed in a nondescript hotel room just off of the interstate. Tomorrow's the funeral, and images flash through my mind.

It's a college summer. I'm standing on a softball field posing for a picture with my teammates. We're arm in arm, we're sweaty, and we're all smiling. We're twelve high school friends who just won a softball championship. I'm standing in the back row. Steve is kneeling in the front. The picture is taken, and we break apart. Time to celebrate. Time to drink. Time to laugh continuously. Time to rehash each and every play over and over again.

Earlier in the evening, as my friend Bill and I drove from the funeral home to the hotel, I reminded him of the picture. He instantly knew which picture I was talking about. I remarked that if someone were to slowly scan each face in that picture and was then asked which one of those young men would die of a heart attack at the age of 44, Steve would have been the last one they would have picked. Without missing a beat, Bill turned to look at me and replied, "They would have picked you." I nod.

I lie in the dark, scanning that picture slowly in my mind, and I ask questions that people ask when someone they love has died. Why do some get to live and some have to die? Why him? Why not me? I continue to stare at the ceiling, unable to sleep. I want to go home. I want to be with my wife and my children.

The night drags on. My brain continues to present a montage of moments from my life with Steve when an unexpected face appears. It's Earlie Mae.

Earlie Mae was the woman who cleaned our house when I was growing up. She was an African-American woman who had grown up in the Deep South. She was probably close to 60 when she first started, and she continued to work for my family for the next 20 years. When she first came to work for my family, my brothers and I didn't pay much attention to her, and we figured that she didn't pay much attention to us. As time passed, we came to realize that she didn't miss a thing. She knew us, in many ways, better than our parents did.

My brother and I are telling Earlie a story about Steve. She smiles, shakes her head slowly, and says, "Poor Little Stevie!" We ask her why she always calls him that, and she replies, "He just so vulnerable." My brother and I lean back and laugh loudly. We shake our heads. Earlie must be crazy - Steve has it all. He's handsome, he's smart, and he's one of the best athletes we know. My brother and I would never actually say these words to each other, but it is understood.

What my brother and I didn't understand then was that Earlie Mae saw something in Steve that most of those around him couldn't. There *was* a vulnerability inside of Steve, and it was exposed, layer by layer, to those of us who were closest to him as he entered the adult world. We came to see that it was very important for Steve to present an image of professional achievement to the world, even when things weren't going very well. More than a few of us from our high school crowd were adrift in the months (and, for some of us, years) that followed our graduating from college, but it bothered Steve much more than it did the rest of us. This would have been all well and good if it wasn't for the sinking feeling I have that Steve might not have allowed himself to see what others saw in him. Did he see the Steve who built others up? Did he see the Steve who brought laughter with him wherever he went? Did he see the Steve who left an impression on everyone he met? Did he regard these qualities as successes?
I continue to lie awake, trying to make sense of Steve's death, looking to a cherished picture and a wise old woman for clues. Maybe if I had seen him more than once in the past 14 years I'd have a better chance.

#

The funeral. I walk into the church. The pastor steps up to stand in front of the congregation with a guitar strapped across his neck, and I start to think that this might be the right man for the job. The pastor welcomes everyone and then plays his guitar while a young man sings a hymn. After the song, the pastor explains that we aren't going to have a formal service. Instead, he invites us to stand up and tell stories about Steve. Now I know for certain that this is the right man for the job.

Stories are told. Some have the crowd roaring in laughter while others bring about a quiet sadness. I am sitting between my two friends, Bill and Dave. Dave turns to me and whispers, "Wild Thing?" I look at him like he's crazy. I turn to Bill sitting next to me, and he just raises his eyebrows in response. I look around the room. I see the pastor with his guitar, and I start to realize that Dave may be a little bit crazy, but it's the brilliant kind of crazy, the "let's seize the day" kind of crazy.

I'm a senior in high school. My dad and my stepmother are going through a trial separation (do those ever work?). Each weekend, my dad goes away to be with my stepmother, leaving me alone in the house. One of the benefits of this arrangement is that I am here, in my house on a Saturday night, surrounded by my closest friends, my favorite beverages, and instruments with amplifiers. It's just about time for me to step up to the mike. I don't play an instrument, and I don't really sing, but one of the traditions of these jam sessions is that I, the host, get up and sing "Wild Thing". I'm called up to the mike. The crowd cheers. I look out into the crowd and I see Steve raising a beer in salute. We rip into the song. It is wild, and it is a thing.

We had dozens of those jam sessions over the course of about three years. I sang "Wild Thing" at just about every one of them, and the song has followed me into my adult life. At my wedding reception, after some persuasion from our friend Weenie, I got up with the band and sang the song to my wife. Now the song is here again, this time at a funeral.

I've had only a few moments to run all of this through my head as I sit here in the pew, but it has become clear that "Wild Thing" is the exact right thing to do. Dave quietly approaches the pastor as someone is telling a story. Dave leans over and speaks in the pastor's ear. The pastor smiles as he nods his head.

So Dave, Bill, and I, joined by the pastor on guitar, stand in front of this packed church. I give a short explanation of what we are going to sing and why. I tell the people looking up at us that we are certain the song, as sung by us, would bring a huge smile to Steve's face. We sing, the audience claps along, and smiles spread out throughout the chapel, the most important ones coming from Steve's wife and kids. I feel the spirit and the sheer power of friendship as I stand up there singing for Steve with Dave and Bill. The lyrics to the song may not have much to do with the present circumstances, but the act of singing has shared our love for Steve, a love that binds this gathering together on this day.

More stories are told, and then a boy who looks to be about 12 years old stands up and tells us about a basketball game. The boy shares that he was not a star player, but that Steve had taken the time to work with him. The boy describes a play where one of his teammates got a rebound. As the boy was heading up the court, he heard Steve shout to him from the stands, "Nice block out!" The boy quietly states that Steve's words "made my day". He sits down.

I know from years of playing basketball that not many people in the stands notice a good block out, much less yell encouragement to the kid who did it. When the boy sits down, I look at the ground and say to myself, "I know that feeling."

I'm on a golf course in DeKalb, Illinois. Steve's parents moved here toward the end of our college days. We're playing golf with some friends Steve has made during his short stay here. I am the world's worst golfer. I have never taken a lesson and have no clue what I'm doing. Hole after hole, I wind up furiously, swing for the fences, top the ball, and watch it roll meekly for, at most, maybe 50 yards. After a few holes, it becomes clear to me that my act is wearing on Steve's buddies - my flailing is slowing their game down.

We move on, and I am getting increasingly frustrated. I swing, swear, and pound my club into the ground. Steve's buddies are becoming increasingly grim and silent. Steve, on the other hand, keeps smiling and gently teases me, trying to get me to lighten up.

Then, on what feels like the 117th hole, I do something right. I get a ball up in the air, it goes in a straight line, and lands on the fairway. There are half-hearted claps and some words of surprise from Steve's buddies, but as I turn

156

to walk back to my bag, I see Steve running at me with a huge smile on his face. He runs straight at me, jumps on me, and hugs me. As we walk down the fairway together, I am grinning. Steve is beaming as he slaps me on the back.

On a planet of billions of people doing billions of things on that day twenty years ago, Steve's reaction to that fluke of a shot was a microscopic moment, but it meant the world to me. It made my day.

The funeral ends. I meet Steve's friends and neighbors at the reception afterwards. Bill, Dave, and I get many compliments for "Wild Thing". After an hour or so, it's time to say goodbye. I want to stay, but it's time to go.

Bill and I are in the car, and we are driving away from Steve. We're quiet. We are heading home to our wives and our children. I think back to a conversation Bill and I had just a few months before.

We're in Bill's kitchen talking about getting the softball team from all those years ago back together. We are as serious as we ever are about getting everyone together, which means that we mean well but neither of us will follow through. We are talking about Steve, wondering where he is and what he is doing. We both share how much we miss him without actually saying that we miss him. I make a decision in my mind that I am going to go home and track down Steve's number and give him a call.

We continue to drive in silence. I watch the highway pass underneath us, and I think back to the days, weeks, and months that went by after that conversation in Bill's kitchen. All of that time. I could have found him. I could have called. But I didn't.

The phone rings. I'm lying on the couch watching television. My wife picks up the phone in the other room. She comes in and hands it to me. The voice on the other end of the line says, "Steve died."

Bill drops me off in front of my house after the long drive. I watch his car lights disappear down the block. I put down my bags and sit on my front porch, thinking. I look up to the sky and I wish that I had had just one more chance to see Steve.

Steve and I are sitting at my kitchen table. I tracked him down, called him, and invited him to drop by if he was ever in town. Our wives are in the living room getting to know one another. Steve's kids are in the basement playing video games with mine. He and I are catching up, laughing about the good times we had and the foolish things we did.

There is a break in the conversation, a moment of reflective silence amongst the laughter. Before I can stop myself, I look at Steve and blurt out the words, "Thank you." He gives me a quizzical look. An excruciatingly awkward moment ensues, followed by some uncomfortable shifting in our chairs. Suddenly Steve bursts into laughter and begins a meandering story that uses many, many words to say what I had foolishly tried to say using only two.

I unlock the front door to my house and step into the front hall. It is dark, and everything is still. I am empty, and yet I am full. I look up the stairs to where my wife, my daughter, and my son are sleeping, and I become aware of just how fragile the foundation of our home feels beneath my feet.

Rapture By Avon

Mike Deller

Brenda had only ever been in a taxi twice before. This time was different though. This time she had actually called it for herself. Fifty-three years ago was the first time, a second in the Queen's Silver Jubilee year, and now today. She looked at the pictures in the frame – Sandra and the boys in front of Sydney Opera House, Sandra and the boys at Ayers Rock. *Maybe I should give her a quick call, just to let her know*, she thought, but the memory of all the other phone calls stayed her hand. The chats that turned into one-sided lectures, with Brenda's protests going unheard. Brenda could almost rehearse her side of the conversation – "*It's only a funny turn, Sandra. I called a taxi because I didn't want to bother the ambulance people. I know it is an extravagance, but it is my money, after all, and a taxi seems a more civilised way to go.*" And then Brenda would have to cut it short with "*Give my love to my grandchildren,*" before things got heated. Sometimes it seemed to Brenda that the roles had been reversed, and that she played the child to Sandra's parent. Perhaps, she thought, Australia is the right place for Sandra. Nine hours and half a world away is about as close as we have ever been.

The friendly *brrapp* of the taxi horn interrupted her thoughts, a pleasing sound, so unlike the yapping cars stuck at traffic lights. She paused in the hall to check in the mirror that the dabs of makeup she had applied were still in place.

It's only hospital, but there's no point looking any worse than you feel, is there? And there might be some handsome doctor who is on the lookout for a woman in her sixties. Fat blooming chance of that. Or of me passing for "in her sixties". The thought raised a weak smile and the old woman in the mirror smiled back at her. *Who are you,* she wondered, *and what are you doing looking back at me like that?*

***

It is 1958. She is looking in the mirror, carefully applying the makeup that inspires such disapproval from Mum. Yardley Double Event lipstick and a tiny dab of Rapture by Avon for behind the ears.

Mum's voice climbs wearily up the stairs. 'I went round to Auntie Vi's today, Brenda. I say, I went round to Auntie Vi's, to see Nanna.'

Here comes a "Nanna" story. Brenda smiles as she touches the edges of her scarlet smile with a tissue.

'Yes, well I was reading Woman's Realm and there was a thing in there about how when if old people are bad tempered and complaining all the time it's because they are, you know, they "can't go", and they said "All-Bran" is the stuff to do the trick, so I went to the shops and got some and your Auntie Vi and me wanted to see if it'd cheer Nanna up. She wouldn't have any of it, anyway. Said she'd go when the good Lord moved her and not a moment before.'

A brief pause, then Mum's knitting needles, and Mum, start up again.

'There's a lovely recipe for "Brisket and Potato Curry" in there. I thought we might have that tomorrow, seeing as it's getting colder these nights.'

Brenda pouts at her reflection in the mirror, and giggles. 'Lovely. All-Bran and curry.' Not so loud that Mum can actually hear her.

'How would you like a cup of tea? A cup of tea and a nice piece of cake?'

'No time, Mum. It's Thursday night.'

'Take It From Here is back on tonight. Stay in and listen to it with me, you know how you like *The Glums.'*

'Thursday is Palais night and that means dancing and friends and...'

'...and boys. Like that Stiff Twitcher you think so much of. Great greasy herbert.'

By now Brenda is at the bottom of the stairs.

'Cliff Richard, Mum. And he's not a herbert he's just... Oh, boy!'

She takes her coat off a peg and puts it on. She pauses to check herself makeup in the mirror.

Mum steps into the hall, catches sight of Brenda's make-up, gives her one of *those* "Like a bloomin' Red Injun" looks, shaking her head.

Then Mum tells her to just be careful out there what with what happened to that girl the other week, and Brenda reminds her that the war's long over, there's no blackout now, she's safe as anything. Mum comes straight back with the start of how 'I met your dad in the blackout, and believe me, Brenda, if the lights had been on, I wouldn't be where I am today,' but Brenda is out of the door and off down the street. Poor old Mum. Life hasn't been easy, even if she does tell everyone that Brenda's father died in the war (and Brenda's mum certainly hopes that he did, because if she ever sees that bugger's face again...)

Brenda turns right out of her gateway, barely noticing the man leaning against the garden wall a few doors down the other way, between the pools of light from the streetlamps, exhaling fag-smoke into the chill night air like an impatient steam-train. And she doesn't notice him toe-twist his cigarette butt, pocket his hands and start walking in the same direction as her, but she hears his steel-tipped footsteps on the pavement, so she picks up her pace very slightly, and it seems to her that perhaps he has done the same, and she glances over her shoulder and there he is, but she can't turn back now, she would have to pass him to get back to her gate, and is he getting closer? And he's not looking at her, it's as if he's tracking her by scent, or sound, and he is, he is getting closer all the time.

There is an audible snap as headlights flare and fill the street with light; a taxi, a beautiful Beardmore, oh thank you God, rolling out of the darkness towards her, pulling up by her side, and the driver has opened his window.

'Hop in, miss.'

'I didn't...'

'I know, miss.'

'But I can't afford...'

'My treat,' he says and she looks back down the street and the man is slouched against a wall once more, matching another fag, looking anywhere but in her direction, so she gets in the taxi which soon pulls up outside the Palais.

'Here we are then. This is your Six-Five Special arriving at, oh, quarter past seven. Not too late, eh?'

She can hear coming from inside the hall the sound of a big band playing jive music.

'Thanks ever so, I don't know...'

'You have fun now, miss. Find yourself a nice young man to walk you home safely,' the driver says, smiling eyes looking at her in his rear-view mirror. 'I'll be waiting outside in case you need me.' He chuckles. 'Don't think there's much chance of that, though. Not tonight.'

She thanks him, and enjoys her evening, and is, in fact, walked home by a very nice young man. As they leave the Palais, she sees the taxi parked outside and gives a discrete finger wave. Its lamps glow like a woken watchdog, then fade. She will see the boy a few times over the next month or so, until it fizzles out as these things do. Some things are for the moment, and some are forever.

***

It is 1977. A party is in progress outside in the street and she can hear Rod Stewart on a record player croaking the big news that the first cut is the deepest, but she knows different; the first cut is just for starters. Her daughter wants them to join in the fun but William (always William, never Bill) tells her she can watch it on telly with them or go to her bloody room. Brenda hands him the

Party Seven that she has just been to the off-license to buy for him. She picks up its already emptied predecessor and turns to take it to the kitchen.

'Change, Brenda?'

Brenda hands him a few small coins which she already has in her hand. He takes the coins from her and carefully counts them in one hand. He catches her wrist firmly in his other hand while he checks the change again. He narrows his eyes and looks suspiciously at her, then releases her.

She takes a magazine from the bag, sits in the other armchair, and starts to read. She keeps her face carefully neutral. She doesn't want to set him off. Not again. Not so soon.

'New magazine?'

'It's last week's. Woman's Realm. Maureen gave it to me. Said she'd finished with it.' The need to elaborate, worried that too little explanation will seem like surliness, too much like insolence, is like fingers round her throat.

William rattles the coins in his hand then puts them in his pocket. 'Huh. Nice woman, that Maureen. More money than she knows what to do with.'

He picks up the can and places it on his lap. He punches a hole in the top of the can with the church-key. Froth pours out over his trousers. Her fault, for hurrying back, shaking the can. But she knew it would have been her fault, too, if she had walked back too slowly.

'Shit.'

William wipes the spilt beer off with his hand, looks round for somewhere to wipe his hand, then wipes his hand on his shirt.

'Shit.'

William pours himself a glass of beer, but overfills the glass. The beer spills onto the carpet.

'Shit, shit, shit.'

Brenda glances in William's direction and (she can't help it, and it is only for a second) she purses her lips briefly and then looks back quickly at her magazine.

'It's only poxy Watney's.'

Silence.

'Brenda?' and now she can hear his breathing, becoming excited and angry. 'I'm talking!'

William very deliberately takes the magazine from Brenda, slowly tears it in half. He puts the ruined magazine on the floor between their chairs. The television is showing Jubilee parties all over the country.

'Reading? When I'm talking, Brenda?'

Spit sticky-mists her face.

'I said; it's only poxy Watney's. I'm hardly going to get pissed on Watney's am I?

She raises a hand to wipe the drops away, but with just his index finger William lowers her hand back into her lap. Gently done, but the touch burns like fear.

'You know why drinking Watney's is like having it off in a rowing boat? Eh?'

It starts like this, and she knows where it goes, she knows the punchline already, so she makes an excuse to leave the room, goes upstairs to the bathroom, and his voice echoes up the stairwell, 'They're both effing close to water,' and his laugh is sandpaper on her soul. She repairs her makeup, the bruise-covering face powder bought with pennies saved by money-off vouchers, enters their bedroom and pulls the small suitcase out from under the bed where it has been for months, already packed with a few essentials for her and Sandra, just in case. She reaches into a drawer and pulls out a dusty, empty, scent bottle, the single souvenir of her carefree days. She wonders how she is going to get down the hall and out the front door without him noticing.

The doorbell rings.

'Get it'. His voice from the back room where the TV displays the happy celebration scenes.

Again, the doorbell.

'Get it. Don't make me...' and she is in Sandra's room, taking her daughter by the hand, shushing her, leading her down the stairs to the front door.

'Well? Who is it?' his voice from deep within the armchair. She opens the front door. There is no-one there. The doorstep is deserted, the road is empty, but at the end of the path the gate is wide open. And then she looks again and in the road outside stands a taxi, engine running, passenger door inviting.

'Come on, Sandra, a little ride,' she whispers and they walk quietly down the path, leaving the door open behind them, fearing the snap of the latch will let him catch them. They settle into the back seat.

'Where to, Missus?'

Brenda panics. She had only thought of departure. Destination... anywhere. She automatically touches the bruise of her face, trying to conceal it.

'A bit "handy", eh? I know just the place, missus. They'll look after you and the young 'un, keep you out of mischief, out of harm's way. They look after a lot of women who have, you know, husbands who get a bit "handy".'

The taxi pulls away.

Brenda turns to take one last look at the house. The front door is closed.

***

Brenda settled herself in the back of the taxi, checking that she had everything she needed for hospital as the vehicle pulled away from the kerb. Handbag, overnight bag, didn't know if she might be kept in, she was feeling very...

'How are you feeling, sweetheart?'

And she realised the poorly feeling was passing, in fact... 'You know, I think it might have been a false alarm. I didn't want to call an ambulance, in case that was all it was.'

'I know, sweetheart, you didn't want to put anyone to any trouble, did you.'

She saw his eyes in the mirror, and they seemed friendly, familiar.

The corners of his eyes wrinkled. A smile that reaches all the ways to his eyes, she thought, that was nice, you didn't see that so much nowadays.

'Perhaps,' she said, 'we might as well turn round and go back home.'

'I don't know, Brenda, what do you reckon?' as he reached up and turned the mirror slightly so that now she could see herself.

'Oh,' she said, and again, 'Oh.' Yardley Double Event made a red circle of her lips. She hadn't worn that colour since... oh, she didn't know when. She raised her hands to touch her face and saw girl's hands, her own hands but seventeen years old again. Manicured, polished nails, pale blue veins tracing the smooth skin, not the knotted strings she had become used to.

She opened her handbag. On the very top of everything else, a scent bottle, filled with pale golden scent, flashed crystalline pins of delight.

'I said I be waiting, didn't I? If you needed me.'

She thought she should feel sad, sorry for Sandra perhaps, but...

'Sandra's big enough to look after herself, and she's got her own family to worry about. You don't need to worry about Sandra any more. You don't need to worry about anything. You just sit back.'

In the distance, Brenda heard the sound of music, a big band playing jive.

'Shall I go dancing?'

'Dancing tonight and every night, for as long as you want,' he said. 'Here, can I do my favourite taxi-driver line?'

She nodded.

'OK, here it is; do you know who I've had in the back of this cab?'

'Go on.'

'Everyone. Abso-bloomin'-lutely everyone.'

And Brenda smiled her Yardley smile and settled back in a haze of Rapture for her last taxi-ride.

Junk

Mandy Huggins

A small tow-haired boy shrieks with delight as he races towards the sea. No more than five years old, and lathe-thin in his baggy shorts, he zigzags down the crowded beach.

I want to watch him scramble between rock pools; parting fronds of seaweed to reveal tiny crabs and the blood red tentacles of sea anemones. I want him to feel the silky softness of a donkey's ear squeezed between chocolatey fingers, and taste the sweet crunch of his first wafer cornet.

His mother leans heavily on the railings, the nub-end of a cigarette nipped tightly between thin lips. She flicks it across the pavement, yelling at him as he disappears down the beach. A voice to topple sandcastles; rasping the sand into submission.

"Get back 'ere *now*, we're goin' for chips!"

He slithers to a halt and turns towards the direction of her voice, hope and excitement draining from his face. He glances at the sea and then back up the beach, weighing the risks. She shouts again, and his skinny frame slumps in defeat.

As he walks back up to the road, she grabs his bucket of treasured shells and empties them onto the sand.

"And you can forget bringing that load o' junk wi' you 'n' all."

My heart flips over, just like when the flight attendant announces the charity collection. I always know it's coming: the sentence that rips my heart out every time.

"Some of these children have never seen the sea."

California

Anastasia Towe

I gripped the armrest and felt my stomach drop as we prepared to land in California. My face was tingling, I felt overheated, and my stomach seemed less than pleased with the experience. My brother slept peacefully next to me, the subtle scent of soap and boy wafting off of his head, and I was once again jealous of his easygoing nature. While he enjoyed his pleasant dreams, I was fighting to keep my lunch down. I won, but just barely. My relief soured soon after we landed and I remembered what was ahead. An entire two weeks with the man I'm obliged to call my father. Just the kind of Christmas vacation I always wanted.

He was standing there when we made our way out of the terminal, with his arms crossed over his chest, his cropped hair, stiff stance, and the intensity of his gaze perfecting the picture of a retired military man. Brian ran ahead to greet our father, but I hung back, taking my time. I wasn't ready to jump for joy at the sight of the man who had threatened to take my mom to court if she didn't ship us across the country. He hadn't bothered to spend time with us when he lived five minutes away, or even before the divorce, despite my efforts. I was tired of hearing the same excuses over and over again, so I had just given up. Then he decided to move to California, and suddenly seeing his children was a big deal to him. Never mind the fact that neither of us had ever flown before.

It was no secret to him that I hadn't wanted to come out here, but his face had softened as we approached, and I smiled in spite of myself when he picked Brian up into a bear hug. It was so much easier to despise him or pretend he didn't exist when he was a thousand miles away.

"Hello, Beth. Welcome to California." He smiled and held out his arms to me, as if he was oblivious to the rift that had opened up between us. It occurred to me that he was honestly trying to bridge that gap, but I knew my father. He could hold a grudge just as well as I could, and I hadn't exactly been the most loving daughter lately. Despite my misgivings, I stepped into the hug. I had already decided to be civil during our visit. Not for his sake, but for Brian's. He was too young to remember the verbal and emotional abuse, and how easily our father had left us without looking back.

"I have a surprise for you guys waiting at the house, so let's get out of here. Brian! Slow down!" He shouted after Bri, who had taken off towards the parking garage, his small carryon bag bouncing around behind him. I followed them at my own pace, listening to the wheels on my suitcase rattle against the tiled floor.

It wasn't until I was sitting in the backseat of his shiny new sports car that I noticed the ring. Bri had called shotgun and I hadn't protested, so I settled into the cramped space in the back. As I looked around the interior of the car, my gaze fell upon my father's hands, resting on the steering wheel. They were large, just like the rest of him, rough and veiny. But that wasn't what my eye was drawn to. It was on the ring finger of his left hand. The band was wide and silver, with grooves encircling the top and bottom edges. It didn't quite fit his finger; the skin bulged on both sides, and I wondered how it wasn't cutting off his circulation. A few second passed before I stopped staring at the ring and began to comprehend its meaning. He hadn't worn his wedding band in years, and besides, the one I remembered from my childhood had been gold. This was a new band.

I stared silently out the window, cutting myself off from the noise of the radio and the traffic, dwelling on the fact that my father had gotten married without telling me. Without telling us. My mother couldn't have known about it either. My face contorted into a scowl and my eyes burned. I glared at the back of his head for a few seconds and then turned away again. He had mentioned a surprise waiting at his house; well this was certainly a surprise. The snow continued to fall outside and I let myself get lost in its swirling patterns.

"So Beth, how has school been? Getting all A's?"

"Sure. It's been fine." I wondered why he was suddenly so interested in my life. Perhaps being married was making him think about being a father again.

"That's a very informative answer there, Beth, thanks for enlightening me. Any other exciting things going on in your life?"

"Nope, not really." I turned to glare at him in the rearview mirror. "How about you? Anything exciting you haven't told us about yet?"

He looked away, and I followed suit. Brian was too enamored with the wintry world outside his window to notice what had just passed between us. Escaping the confines of this car was the first thing on both of our minds.

The house was unremarkable, and my mind was too overwhelmed by the thought of meeting my stepmother to give it much consideration anyway. I did notice the other car in the driveway though, a powder blue punch buggy.

"Punch buggy! No punch back!" Brian shouted at me as he turned around in his seat to punch my arm before jumping out of the car.

"You guys get your bags from the trunk, you each have your own room," he said as he walked into the house. Brian grabbed his suitcase and ran off after him, excited as ever. I dragged my feet and slammed the door when I got in. While Brian ran off to investigate his room, I decided to confront my father.

"So...where is this surprise you were talking about? Or I suppose a better question would be, where's your wife?" I stood in the front hallway with my arms crossed, glaring at the back of his head. He pretended not to hear me.

"Come on Dad, I saw your ring. I suppose it would have been too much to tell your children you were getting married, let alone invite them to the wedding. Not that I would have gone."

He finally turned around to face me, and I was surprised by the pleading expression on his face. "Beth, please try to be civil. Karrie really wants you guys to like her. I want you guys to like her. She's a great woman. She should be back from walking the dog any minute."

"Oh, so her name's Karrie. That's nice to know. Well when she gets here you can tell her I went to bed early. Nothing personal, it's just been a long day. Goodnight." I didn't stick around long enough to see his expression change, but I knew it would. That look would have been more familiar; his anger was no stranger to me. But I was surprised that he didn't tell me to stop right then, to come back and apologize, to stop being a selfish brat. He didn't say a word.

It had been too late for me to call my mom that night because of the time difference, so I called her as soon as I woke up the next morning and told her about Karrie. The house was empty, so I sat in the front room, watching Brian play in the snow. Karrie was probably out there keeping an eye on him since my father was at work, but I couldn't see her.

"Mom, I don't know if I can take this. I mean, who does that? Who gets married and doesn't even tell his kids? And he expects me to be ok with it? To like her? I've never even met this woman before, and now she's my stepmother!"

"Honey, I don't like it any more than you do, but I can't do anything. You understand don't you? I would fly out there myself and bring you home if I could, you know that. You have to be strong. Find something to do to occupy yourself, and you'll be home before you know it."

"But what am I supposed to do? I can't just avoid her for two weeks; I'll have to talk to her eventually."

"I know honey, I know. Try to just think of her as your dad's friend instead of his new wife, and try to be nice. Your father should have told you, yes, but you shouldn't take your disappointment in him out on this woman. I love you Beth, and I know you'll be ok. You're my daughter after all. How is your brother doing?"

I sniffed as I told her how excited and oblivious Bri was. He was playing outside in the snow; I could see him through the window, making snowballs in the front yard. I just wanted this to be over, but my mom was right. I could fight through it. She always knew how to comfort me. Brian ran in, covered with snow and jabbering about his snow angel, just as I was hanging up.

"Bri, you're going to drip everywhere! Go put your coat away and clean yourself off!"

"Don't tell me what to do Beth, you're not the boss of me," he said, and then proceeded to run around the room, flinging the melting snow everywhere. *Great*, I thought to myself, *and I'll probably get in trouble for letting him do this.* And then I heard her coming.

"Brian! Your father wouldn't want you to – oh. Beth, you're up. Good morning."

I took a moment to take in this first sighting of my new stepmother. She was short, probably shorter than me, and had her dark hair tied back in a low ponytail. I was relieved to see that she looked to be about the same age as my mom.

"Hello Karrie." I tried to do what my mom had suggested, just pretend she was a friend. It was easier said than done.

She turned her attention to Brian for a moment. "Brian, your father wouldn't want you to track snow through the house. Go take your coat off and hang it by the door."

I watched him do as she said, wondering why he would so quickly obey this stranger before his own sister, but I tried to shrug it off.

She turned back to me, trying to hide her obvious discomfort. "So...Beth...how are you liking California so far?"

"I wouldn't really know, it's only been one night. The snow looks nice though."

"Yes, the snow is great this time of year. Not fun to drive in though. Well, I should go – " Her eyes shifted to the front hallway.

"Wait. I have a question for you. How long have you been married to my father?"

She gave me a quizzical look. "We got married in August, you know that."

"Actually, no, I didn't know that. I didn't even know my father was remarried until yesterday."

"He didn't...he didn't tell you? Oh Beth, I'm so sorry, this must be a terrible shock for you, I –"

"It's fine Karrie, it's not your fault. Listen, I've got some schoolwork to do while I'm here, so I'm going to go do that. I guess I'll see you at dinner."

"Oh, ok. Yes, I'll see you then." I could feel her watching me as I went back to the bedroom and closed the door. Later that night, as I doodled at the bottom of a page in my journal, I heard raised voices coming from the bedroom that she shared with my father. I took some small satisfaction in knowing that she was upset with him too.

My father had to work for most of the first week that Brian and I spent in California, while we stayed at the house. I hadn't asked him about his job, so I didn't know much, just that he worked with sonar and usually had long hours. Bri got his fill of playing in the snow with Karrie watching him, and I kept myself occupied with reading, homework, and journaling. I had been writing my thoughts down every day for almost a year, ever since my grandma had given me this red marbled journal with gold-trimmed pages for Christmas. Usually I just did it out of habit, but now it seemed like a necessity. It would keep me from exploding.

It seemed that my friends were all too busy for phone or text conversations, so I barely talked to anyone besides my mother. She called every night to see how I was doing, and I vented to her about my self-imposed isolation. I was obligated to leave my room for meals, but I kept silent during them. The only time I saw my father was at dinner, and he usually left me alone.

It was on the fourth day of our visit that I finally decided to listen to what my mom had been telling me the past few nights: stop moping and make the best of the situation. So I joined Karrie and Brian for lunch, and tried to be sociable.

"So Bri, what did you make in the snow today?"

"I made a fort! And then I hid behind it and I threw snowballs at Karrie. She tried to get me back, but my fort kept me safe. It was awesome." He beamed at me and then at Karrie. I couldn't help but smile back.

"Sounds like you guys have been having fun. Maybe I'll join you out there tomorrow."

"Really? That would be so cool Beth! We could have a snowball war, and you could build your own fort!" He looked so excited that I began to regret keeping myself separate from them for the past few days. I had forgotten that by shutting myself off from Karrie and my father, I was shutting him out too.

"Yeah, Bri. It'll be great." I looked over at Karrie to see her smiling at me.

"You know, it's a shame that you guys won't get to meet John and Sarah, I think you would get along. They would have loved to have a snowball war. They're spending the holidays with their father too."

"Who?" I could feel the happiness from the previous moment starting to slip away.

"John and Sarah? My kids?" She saw the expression on my face and her eyes widened. "Oh.

Your...your father hadn't told you about them yet, had he? Oh I'm sorry, I didn't mean to-"

"Wait, you have *kids*? And you said they're spending the holidays with their father, so...have they been living here?"

"Well...yes. I mean, those are their rooms." She nodded towards the bedrooms where Brian and I had been sleeping.

I stared at her for a moment. "Well that's," I paused for a moment to stifle the quiver in my voice, "Great. Just great. You know, I think I'm going to go check out that wonderful snow."

I grabbed my coat and tried not to slam the door on my way out.

The sun reflected back into my eyes so brightly that it hurt, but it was beautiful still. I had never seen the world so covered in snow before. It coated the ground, the trees, the houses, and made everything sparkle and glow in the morning light. If there was anything that could make me feel like this trip wasn't quite as horrible, it was this. The thoughts that were running through my head in that moment were calmed by the quiet serenity of the view around me. Brian and I never did have our snowball war. Instead, I took long walks in this wintry dream for the next few days while Karrie watched him build snowmen and forts in the front yard. The days bled together into images of white and gold.

Suddenly our first week in California was ending and it was the weekend again. It was the first day since we had been there that my father didn't have to work, which of course only gave me more reason to spend it outside, away from the house. I had heard Karrie confront him the other night about all the secrets he had been keeping from his own children, but I hadn't been able to make out his excuses. I just knew I would rather be anywhere else than around him.

I was coming back from a long walk in the snow, wanting to stay outside, but needing to eat something before I passed out. Karrie and Brian were outside, and I was hoping to slip inside, grab some food, and get to "my" room before they came in. Lunch with Karrie was something I avoided at all costs.

I plundered the kitchen and then walked to the room, but stopped short in the doorway. My father was standing there with his back to me, leaning on the desk. He had something in his hand.

"What are you doing?"

He turned around so quickly that he dropped what was in his hand. My journal fell to the floor, the pages crumpling. I stared at it, and then back at him.

"Beth, I-"

"Seriously?! You were reading my journal? What is wrong with you?" I stooped to snatch it up off the ground and then glared at him.

"Don't talk to me like that. You've been shutting me out all week; I wanted to know what was going on. Karrie told me that she mentioned John and Sarah, but you never brought it up."

"Well maybe if you had told me yourself instead of trying to hide it you would have gotten my reaction first hand!"

"Don't you reprimand me Beth, remember who is the parent here? I'm not one of your friends that you can just yell at when you get angry!"

"Oh, so you're a parent now. I thought you had excused yourself from that role when you left us. You have no right to invade my privacy like that! If I wanted to talk to you, I would have."

"Well you certainly voiced your opinion well in there!" He started to recite lines from my journal entries, a bitter edge creeping into his voice and his face getting redder with each word *"I can't believe he dragged us all the way out here...I wish I never had to see him again...I hope Karrie knows what she's getting into...He doesn't deserve us, let alone another family."*

I stared at the familiar sight of my father's red face – familiar, yes, but it had never been directed at me before. I don't know how my mother stood it all those years. My anger boiled in my cheeks, I could feel them tingling.

"Yeah? And I meant every word of it! What kind of father doesn't tell his children that he's getting married, let alone that he's been married for four months? Or that his new wife has kids of her own, and that he's building a happy new family after leaving his own kids behind and moving across the country?"

I watched as the ugly purple vein in his forehead pulsed, and began to feel old memories tugging at the back of my mind. *This isn't going to end well for you.* My own fury began to fade, and was replaced with a deep sorrow. I was surprised to see that his expression began to change to. As I watched, the blood stopped rushing into his face and he looked down.

"You know what, Beth? Maybe you should just go home. That's clearly what you want. I'll get you a plane ticket, drive you to the airport, and you can just leave."

I stared at him in shock for a moment, but then I shrugged. "Fine. I don't know why you made me come here in the first place. You don't seem to want to include me in your new life anyway."

He walked past me and through the doorway, not looking back. "Just get your stuff packed. You're leaving tomorrow."

My eyes stung and the look on Bri's face as he watched me walk towards security at the airport nearly broke me. I tore myself away from the gaze of his sad brown eyes. I couldn't stand to leave him alone, not like this. But I refused to cry there in front of him, and I wouldn't give my father the satisfaction of knowing I cared at all. The tears came slowly as I wound my way through the security line, sliding down my cheeks one at a time. They continued as I made my way to the gate and boarded the plane. With the bitter realization that I had gotten what I wished for, I looked out the window as the plane took off and gazed down at the small piece of northern California that I was leaving behind. I had a feeling that I wouldn't be coming back.

Authors Notes

Byron Jones is from the future. It was an accident. He misses being able to walk on water and holidaying on Mars. However, he has always been a history buff and he revels in the quaint ways of this century. Through creative writing he hopes to convey a message to the future that he is ok.

David Rowland is a retired psychiatric nurse living in Cornwall. *The Saboteur* was based on an idea that came to him in a supermarket queue whilst ruminating on the mechanics of the consumer economy. As well as writing short stories he writes and performs his own songs with his partner, poet Abigail Wyatt and also enjoys amateur dramatics. He has a Masters Degree in Art History and is looking forward to one day spending a bit more time in the garden.

Jim Meirose's work has appeared in numerous magazines and journals, including *Collier's Magazine*, *The Fiddlehead*, *Witness*, *Alaska Quarterly Review*, and *Xavier Review*, and has been nominated for several awards. Two collections of his short work have been published and three novels are available from Amazon. A fourth novel will be released in 2015 by Montag Press.

Mike Deller is currently engaged on secret work behind enemy lines. Mike has been selected for the first manned Mars mission. Mike is semi-retired from an uninspiring job processing data. Two of these are lies; pick your own truth.

Eryk Pruitt is a screenwriter, author and filmmaker living in Durham, NC with his wife Lana and cat Busey. His short films FOODIE and LIYANA, ON COMMAND have won several awards at film festivals across the US. His fiction appears in *The Avalon Literary Review, Pulp Modern, Thuglit,* and *Zymbol,* to name a few. In 2013, he was a finalist for Best Short Fiction in *Short Story America* and has been nominated for two *Pushcart Prizes* for 2014. His novel *Dirtbags* was published in April 2014, and *HASHTAG* will be published by 280 Steps in May, 2015. A full list of credits can be found at *erykpruitt.com*

Bob Carlton lives and works in Leander, Texas.

Mandy Huggins writes short fiction and travel articles, and can often be found scribbling in notebooks on trains and planes. Her work has been published in anthologies, literary journals, daily newspapers and mainstream magazines.
Mandy has won several writing competitions and been listed and placed in numerous others, including those run by *New Writer, Lightship Publishing, Fish, Ink Tears, English Pen, The Telegraph,* and *Bradt Travel Guides/Independent on Sunday.* She won the *British Guild of Travel Writers New Travel Writer Award 2014* and the Shortest Story category of the *Words with Jam 2014 Short Story Competition.*

Robert Watts Lamon lives in Durham, North Carolina. His short stories have appeared in print and online magazines, including *Toasted Cheese, Foliate Oak, Wild Violet, Xavier Review,* and *The MacGuffin*. He's also contributed an essay and several book reviews to *Liberty (libertyunbound.com)*.

Anthony Rowe lives in Glenview, IL. He is happily married and is the proud father of two children. He is a fifth grade teacher who enjoys writing short stories and essays. You can read them at *byanthonyrowe.com*. The story *Seei---ng Steve* was inspired by the life and premature death of an exceptional friend.

Diya Gangopadhyay I am a writer by passion originally from India and living in New York for the past two years. In my professional life I am an Interaction Designer, working to make technology easier for people to use. I love creative thinking, music, books and debating. Also in love with the great city I live in. You can find more of my work on my blog https://diyaiit.wordpress.com on various things that strike a chord with me.

Allen Kopp lives in St. Louis (hot in summer and cold in winter), Missouri, USA, with his two cats. He has had over a hundred short stories published and expects (hopes) to have many more. He knows that writing fiction is like playing the piano: the more you do it, the better you get at it. His Facebook page is at https://www.facebook.com/allen.kopp.5. His little slice of the blogosphere is at www.literaryfictions.com

Marian Brooks has begun to write some short fiction. Her work has appeared in *Word Riot, The Linnet's Wings, Short Humor Site, Bewildering Stories* and others. She lives in Pennsylvania with her husband and children who have inspired her more than they'll ever know.

Claire Bluett (nee Williams) works, sleeps, and makes merry in Houston, Texas, where she has never once encountered Beyonce unfortunately. She owes Professor Gabriela Maya many thanks for introducing her to Natalia Ginzburg.

Read More Short Stories:

3 MILLION STORIES

THE BEST INTERNATIONAL SHORT STORIES FROM THE OMSCWP 2011

ONE MILLION STORIES SMALL PRESS: BEST OF 2011